Mark's reque
frisson of exci
within Katy.

In a strange sort of w...

regarding her fluctuating emotions in his presence. After all, he was asking for her help, and it seemed that the woman in his life was something of a thorn in his side. She still didn't understand the suddenness of it after two years of having no interest whatsoever in the opposite sex.

Sceptics would say that that was the very reason she had been drawn to him, but Katy knew better!

Frances Crowne's nursing career was set aside for marriage and three children, yet left a sense of thwarted ambition. Later a secretarial career at an agricultural college was followed by freelance writing of romantic fiction and articles for women's magazines. A chance remark at a party led to her writing her first medical stories. Now woven with romance, her nursing ties have come full circle in a most gratifying way.

Recent titles by the same author:

DR WENTWORTH'S BABIES

A MIDWIFE'S CHALLENGE

BY

FRANCES CROWNE

MILLS & BOON®

All the characters in this book have no existence outside the imagination of the author, and have no relation whatsoever to anyone bearing the same name or names. They are not even distantly inspired by any individual known or unknown to the author, and all the incidents are pure invention.

First published in Great Britain 1997
Harlequin Mills & Boon Limited,
Eton House, 18-24 Paradise Road, Richmond, Surrey TW9 1SR

ISBN 0 263 80050 4

Set in Times 10 on 10½ pt. by
Rowland Phototypesetting Limited
Bury St Edmunds, Suffolk

03-9703-53537-D

Printed and bound in Great Britain
by Mackays of Chatham PLC, Chatham

CHAPTER ONE

ROSEWALL GENERAL HOSPITAL lay basking in the warmth of the September sunshine which lingered over the rose gardens, the evocative fragrance of the blooms wafting lazily through the open windows of the senior staff common room.

Katy Woods, midwife and newly appointed ward sister, was enjoying the peace of a short tea-break from Fortune Ward, where they were not exactly rushed off their feet at present with patients giving birth, but a more mundane job was under way: that of redecorating the wards. This necessitated each pair of wards being brought into one while the renovations were carried out, causing both staff and patients to wilt under the inconvenience and reduced space which was so unusual at the Rosewall.

Katy gave a small sigh and rested her head back in the armchair, allowing the buzz of conversation at the other end of the long room to fade into the background as she closed her eyes and relaxed. The moment she did so the wretched sensation came back to her. It was an intense feeling of being perched on the brink of something about to happen. It had been with her now for the last few days. Perhaps she was heading for some kind of sickness from an unpleasant bug. Yet, she felt as fit as fiddle. . .

A sudden crescendo of laughter came from the other end of the room, causing her to open her eyes again. Katy glanced briefly at the three doctors whom she knew, as the other, a stranger, was being given a welter of good-humoured advice.

Men were perverse creatures. Whenever they got

together they acted like schoolboys, or members of a rugger team, splitting their sides at their own jokes. But then, men were not at the top of her priority list at the moment, anyway. . .

'Hi, Katy.' Her friend, Joanna Bennett, from Accident and Emergency, came bounding in suddenly, flopping into the chair at her side. 'You're just the one I wanted to see!'

'Hi! Jo, if you came to borrow some money—sorry, I'm skint too!' Katy grinned, thoroughly awake now.

'No, nothing like that! You know we're expecting a replacement for Professor Mason? Has he arrived yet? I haven't seen him, but my spies tell me he's extremely dishy!'

Katy grinned again, her fair hair gleaming in a long, thick plait as she turned to give a cheeky lift of her smooth eyebrows to the friend with whom she had first started at Rosewall. 'Well,' she said, as if giving the question a great deal of thought, 'you wouldn't have seen him simply because, I believe, he's only been with us for an hour or two—'

Katy broke off, suddenly hearing a scuffing of chairs across the thick green carpet. 'Now,' she murmured, eyes twinkling, as the man whose back had been turned towards her rose from his chair. At least six feet four inches tall, he threw his head back with laughter and strode confidently from the room with his three colleagues. 'Your luck's in,' Katy continued. 'I'm pretty certain it was the tall one in the light grey suit.'

Joanna's round, baby-doll face was a picture as her large brown eyes followed the male retinue. 'You mean the one with the tan? I don't believe it.'

'Well, that's the only new man I've seen here today,' Katy assured her, glancing at the wall clock as she stood up to return to the ward.

Joanna was still sitting virtually open-mouthed. 'Why is it on A and E we always seem to get doctors as old as my father, or young as boy scouts. . . ?' She lowered her voice slightly, as at that moment Miss Munro, the senior nursing officer, entered, speaking in confidential tones to several dignitaries on their way from a board meeting that had been in progress all afternoon. Joanna, nevertheless, pressed on. 'So you think that's Mr Mark Hammond?'

'Yes, I believe so.'

'You lucky thing. You will actually be working with him, the senior consultant on Gynae and Obs, then?'.

'Apparently.'

'You know, you're a cool customer, Katy, it baffles me how you manage it.'

'Well, first of all you simply tell yourself that not all men are gods! After that, it's easy. . .comparatively!' Katy said with feeling. She knew her friend's predilection for anything even mildly resembling the male of the species, so Joanna's extravagant remarks over any new male member of staff were never any surprise to her. Even so, Katy had to admit to being rather impressed herself by the man's appearance as he had walked past her—the confident, leisurely stride, the almost perfect profile but for a shapely nose that might have been in contact with a boxer's glove or a football boot. But when he laughed the slight defect was barely noticeable. . .

Her thoughts were beginning to run riot. Perhaps this Mark Hammond would bring a breath of fresh air to their department. Professor Mason was a pet but did rather tend to be fussy for no apparent reason, usually following his fussiness with a spontaneous lecture on the pitfalls of impatience. That was his hobby-horse.

It would be interesting to discover Mr Mark Hammond's little human failings; presumably he had some, like most people. He was due to conduct his first round on the gynae and obs section in the morning, accompanied by Miss Ursula Munro for formal introductions.

Katy realised Joanna was speaking and glancing at her fob-watch. 'Hey, look at the time! I still have to go to the shop for some tights. I promised that part-time Sister Lake I told you about that I'd only be ten minutes. Just because she's an ex-army nurse, she thinks she can tell us all what to do. See you later!'

Katy smiled to herself. Staff Nurse Joanna Bennett was an excellent nurse but did rather tend to place people into categories, she thought as she stopped on her way back to Fortune to collect any post—not a difficult task when generally new mothers stayed only one or two nights following a normal birth.

'Just a couple for Fortune, Sister. . .'

The pretty young redhead behind the reception desk threw Katy a smile, holding out two letters. 'Hot today, isn't it?'

'Certainly is, Margaret,' she said, taking the letters. 'Have you heard anything yet about having those tonsils out?'

'No, nothing. My boyfriend says he's booking our holiday whether I've heard or not; he's fed up with waiting. No more than I am I can tell you. Ten months is no joke, is it?'

Later, in the dining room, Katy and Joanna were finishing their meal together before returning to duty until ten that night. Their conversation was still about men, Joanna now reflecting upon Ron Green, one of the male nurses who had recently been promoted to charge nurse. She said rather dolefully, 'You don't like him much, do you, Katy?'

Katy shrugged her slim shoulders. 'I can take him or leave him. Maybe you know him better than me; you've worked with him off and on, haven't you?'

'Sure. He's not bad. The only thing is he's coarse at times and thinks he's clever with it. My opinion is that he's too good-looking in a conceited sort of way, and since his promotion he thinks he can walk on water.'

Katy grinned. 'So I gather he's not on your gold list of potential suitors?'

'No fear. He's not my type. I was just interested to know what you thought. Strange, though, isn't it? All the old ladies on his ward love him, won't have a word said against him, apparently.'

'One thing he's good at and that's buttering people up when he wants something. Especially the girls.'

'Do me a favour.' Joanna grinned. But, all the same, Katy did not fail to miss the slight rise of colour in her friend's cheeks.

Katy sipped her tea, gazing through the window at the quiet tranquillity of the summer evening. 'Well, at least he isn't married,' she remarked with a heavy emphasis she hadn't intended, then added more lightly, 'As far as we know, anyway.'

'I'd soon know with any guy. Don't worry, there are no flies on me! I couldn't imagine either you or me getting caught like that,' Joanna said with firm conviction.

'The solution is to take everything a man says with a pinch of salt,' Katy said casually with a laugh. 'That way you may not get hurt.'

Joanna's bright brown eyes were suddenly dreamy. 'How old do you think that new senior gynae character is?'

'Could be forty, but looks a lot younger when he laughs. I'd say he's about thirty-six, maybe thirty-eight.' Katy smiled. 'Actually, I heard that he's around that age.'

'Well, what could be better? You and I are both twenty-six and single . . . Hey, talk of the devil!'

Mark Hammond had just strolled in with Miss Munro, each in animated conversation as a waitress hurried to serve their evening meal.

Katy glanced at them, saying, 'Well, at least he seems to have a good sense of humour. He's even making Ursula smile and that's saying something.'

'Yes, I think he's OK. By the way, what are you doing tonight? How about coming to my room for coffee? My mum sent me one of her fruit-cakes yesterday; it smells gorgeous.'

'I'd love to, Jo, but it's getting late and as soon as I come off duty I have to make a phone call.'

'Well, just have another cuppa.' She looked up from the teapot she was pouring, giving Katy an impish grin. 'Ringing anyone nice? You're always so cagey about your love life, Katy. I wish I could be like you; trouble with me is, I spill everything out.'

Katy laughed. 'That's because you haven't yet met the right man. If you had you'd want to keep it to yourself for a while.'

'Is that why you don't tell me much, then?' Joanna giggled at the closed look on Katy's face. 'No, forget I said that; I promise I won't ask any more personal questions. Unless, of course, you desperately want to tell me who you're ringing later?'

'My brother, actually. He returns to Brussels tomorrow.'

'Oh. . . How is Ross? Still overworked in that legal set-up of his?'

Katy smiled ruefully. ''Fraid so, but he's determined to keep his wife, Fleur, in a decent clinic while she continues with these tests.'

Joanna sighed. 'It's such a rotten shame. They've only been married about six months, haven't they?'

'Yes, and for the last three it's been nothing but trips to the specialists.'

'How will she manage with Ross away?'

'She'll go down and stay with Mum in Clacton, I hope. . .'

The final few hours of Katy's shift went quickly

enough and as soon as she could she hurried downstairs to the telephones, still thinking of thirty-year-old Fleur, so strikingly attractive, so brave, and yet at the moment with her entire career as a fashion buyer for a London store in jeopardy, not to mention her life. . .

'Heck!' To her utter consternation, she had collided with. . .Mark Hammond! 'Oh, I'm so sorry,' she gasped, staring up into the darkest blue eyes that she had ever seen, embarrassment following when she saw his expression was one of great amusement.

'No, please don't apologise,' his rich, deep voice replied. 'My fault entirely. You must take the booth. I'm afraid my mind was not wholly upon what I was doing. . .'

His gaze went over her trim figure clad in light blue, the darker belt and coveted silver buckle enhancing the very pleasant picture she made standing before him. There was a lost look about her. The vivid blue eyes and wheat-coloured hair were such a contrast to the beauties who had held little interest for him when he'd worked in Brunei. Impatiently he put a stop to the random thought. Wasn't it that kind of thinking that had been the beginning of his attraction for Janine. . . ?

The girl was now about to move into the phone booth, although hesitantly. 'Do go ahead, Sister. . .um?' He had raised a sleek, dark eyebrow, not knowing whom he was addressing.

To Katy's intense annoyance she could hardly think of her own name, so conscious was she of his interested perusal; those eyes particularly were almost mesmerising.

'Woods. . .er. . .Katy Woods.' Her confusion wouldn't have been so acute had he been less tall and she hadn't had to tilt her head back to answer him. It put her at a distinct disadvantage, which was rare, given that she was five feet nine inches herself. Hurriedly she gathered her wits together, saying briskly, 'Please. . .'

and indicating that she still preferred him to take the booth.

A slow, lazy smile reached his eyes. 'Thank you, Katy Woods, but no, I would much prefer you went ahead of me! It isn't anything that can't wait anyway.' His deep-set, intelligent eyes twinkled suddenly. 'Maybe yours is!' The implication that she might be ringing a boyfriend was patently obvious. What a joke, she thought with irony as she rang her brother's UK office.

'Hi, Ross. It's Katy!' She loved her only brother deeply and it hurt her so much to hear the sadness in his voice as he answered her question.

'Well, Katy, it's as we thought, I'm afraid. Fleur has to go into the clinic again this week for one further test. If this one's positive, it means a mastectomy of the right breast.'

Katy's heart lurched with misery. How difficult it was to think of something even mildly comforting to say to a loved one. 'In a way it might be a good thing, Ross, after all this time of not knowing. She'll be fine now, you'll see. . .'

'Look, funny face,' Ross said, using his pet childhood name for her, 'I'll give Fleur and Mum your love and tell them you'll keep in touch. I have to hurry now, I'm afraid. I must get back home to Fleur, and once I've taken her into the clinic tonight I'm leaving on a late flight to Brussels. Now, are you OK? Do you think you're going to make a go of this promotion to ward sister, love? It's been so tough for you in the last two years, and, you being you, I suppose you haven't told a soul there about the bigamy. You're doing so damned well, I'm really proud of you, Katy. Dad would have been too if he'd been here. . .'

A lump rose in Katy's throat when she thought of her dear dad who had died suddenly of a heart attack. She took a deep breath, trying to steady her voice.

'Ross,' she said lightly, 'OK, I know its been rough for all of us lately, but there's no need to worry about me; I'm handling it! Don't forget I'm not the first girl in the world to have made a terrible mistake and got over it. Now, you just take care of yourself, and try not to worry. Mum will look after Fleur, and I'll see you when you get back.'

'With a bit of luck, sweetheart, I'll be back early—if I can make it.'

They said their goodbyes, and as she left the telephone Katy noticed that Mark Hammond had managed to find one for himself. He seemed to be engaged in a very animated conversation, his face serious, even angry, and he clearly didn't notice her going past. Katy returned to her ward, pondering on how first impressions were not always right.

The gynae and obs department consisted of one pair of gynaecology wards, one pair of obstetrics, an intensive care baby unit, a large airy nursery for healthy babies, a suite of labour rooms, operating theatres, relatives' overnight accommodation, and all the utility rooms.

Katy's domain was the maternity section known as Fortune Ward. The benefactor who had financed the building of the new section had dedicated it to the memory of his wife, who had died in childbirth. And he'd called it fortune because a rumbustious ancestor of his had captained the tea clipper of the same name and founded an extremely successful firm of insurance brokers which was still very much in business today.

This was the reason why the Rosewall now had one of the best maternity units in the south-east of England. Today, the great sailing ships no longer put into the bustling port of Maldon to offload their cargo, but the area was famed for its oyster beds, and more recently for a leisure-boat marina.

'Oh, Katy, I'm so glad you're back,' Staff Nurse

Tessa Bailey said when she saw Katy arrive, practically bumping into her in the corridor, where comparative silence reigned now that most of the healthy babies—six at present—had just finished their six o'clock feed. 'I can't find young Yvonne Smith anywhere!'

Katy frowned. 'What do you mean? She only had her baby last night. Professor Mason said she should spend another two days here with us at least!'

Tessa all but wrung her hands. 'Oh, hell, I feel it's all my fault! You see, early this afternoon, just prior to the meeting, she asked if I could let her have one of the bedside phones. Naturally I said she could. Meanwhile, I was with Mrs Hall, who was already into her first stages of labour since the induction. There was only Sandra, the new student nurse, on duty for a short while on her own. Apparently after Yvonne had finished her call she told Sandra she was going along to the toilet. When she didn't return, Sandra checked in the nursery, to be told by one of the auxiliaries that Yvonne had been given permission to sit with the child in the sun lounge for a while. She was not there. I reported it to Security and Miss Munro—'

'How long ago was this?' Katy interjected quickly.

'About an hour ago now. Unfortunately the security people had just changed shifts and no one had noticed anything unusual.'

Tessa looked thoroughly miserable with herself, and Katy placed a reassuring hand on her shoulder. 'Well, my bet is that Yvonne's decided to do her own thing and go into the garden with the baby as it's such a warm evening, despite our rules for patients. I'll go downstairs and see if anyone knows anything.'

The phone rang noisily. Katy picked up the receiver. 'Sister Woods. . .'

'Miss Munro here, Sister. About Yvonne Smith. Her boyfriend has just rung in to say that Yvonne and the baby are not coming back to the hospital. He apparently picked them up at one of our more concealed garden entrances and intends taking them up to his mother in Scotland—that's his story, anyhow. I reminded him that Yvonne still needs medical care, and she's to get in touch with a doctor as soon as she can once she arrives.'

Katy groaned. 'I had a feeling something like that would happen, Miss Munro. The girl seemed uneasy after her boyfriend left last night. He was certainly very much on edge. I assumed it had to do with it being his first child, and having been present at the final stage of the birth.'

'Yes, I know what you mean, but we cannot prevent people from discharging themselves, as you know. We can only trust that the wee one is well cared for,' Miss Munro said quickly, her Scottish ancestry coming to the fore when she was agitated. 'I must say, we probably haven't heard the last of her. Pity Mr Hammond doesn't officially begin his duties until the morning. Still, I suppose once he's been told there's little more he can do.'

When Katy went off duty that evening it was still not quite dark. The air seemed soft and warm, above was scattered a lavish shower of stars, and her mind went back to Fleur and her brother, Ross. They were not the only ones with troubles. Even Yvonne, a girl of just seventeen with her newborn child, already appeared to have made a faulty start in life. Gossip had gone around the ward that she and her boyfriend were in some kind of trouble with the police, and now it seemed it might be true.

Slowly she strolled across the immaculate gardens towards the nurses' home, yet she was reluctant to go inside; the pungent scent of the late summer night still lingered and was like balm to her thoughts.

Making up her mind suddenly, she walked past the large double doors of the entrance hall, through a small wicket-gate leading away from the boundary of the marina and strolling holiday-makers. Soon she reached the end of the sea-wall near a beach of sorts, where the sea regularly crept into the estuary and up river, leaving small pools and creeks when the tide receded.

She loved this quiet place, it was always different. The sea was the dominating factor and there was a slightly menacing atmosphere of mystery. Even now, illicit cargo could be smuggled in under cover of darkness. At present the River Blackwater was shining here and there, night and day merging in the uncertain light. She slowed down, watching little spurts of sand showering before her feet where she walked in between stretches of pebbles and relics of old stone jetties, which were revealed only when the tide was low.

Katy shivered slightly—autumn must already be waiting in the wings, she thought. She pressed on towards an outcrop of rock where the estuary widened into the inhospitable arms of the North Sea. For a few moments she stood gazing out across the water, which was grey now, harsh and demanding. Abruptly Katy turned her back on it and began to retrace her steps, when to her surprise she saw the figure of a man strolling nonchalantly along the shallow water's edge. Surely it wasn't Mark Hammond. . .?

But it had to be, there was no mistaking that tall, elegant figure, despite his casual wear in dark jeans and polo-necked sweater. The rhythmic swish of her footsteps must have alerted him, for suddenly he swung round, and on recognising her he lifted a hand in salute.

'Hi!' He grinned, strolling towards her. 'Is this a favourite walk of yours?'

'It is, as a matter of fact,' she answered, feeling rather foolish in her working gear with a navy cardigan tied around her waist. 'Just the sort of night when one can't wait to be part of it.'

'Dcfinitely!' His features were chiselled in the

waning light; his eyes, meeting hers as he spoke now, had a controlled friendliness. 'You know, for me, this is like renewing my childhood days. I spent so many happy hours here that being sent back to school was almost a penance!'

'This must be a wonderful place to grow up in.'

'Indeed.' He nodded. 'And you? You were born in this part of the world?'

'No, the Lowlands of Scotland. My mother only moved here when my father died a few years ago. My brother and I wanted her to be closer to us, and as we both worked in the south it seemed the obvious thing to do.'

He smiled. 'Of course, I realise now; I had noticed that attractive lilt in your voice, but having lived abroad for so long, I'm not so quick at spotting regional differences.'

'Actually my father was English,' she said. 'He went into partnership with a friend running a boat-building yard. We lived at Kirkcaldy on the east coast of Scotland until he retired. Later we moved closer to Edinburgh, by which time Ross and I had established lives of our own, of course—'

Katy broke off suddenly. Why on earth was she chattering on to this man, about whom she knew almost nothing? Yet he asked no questions when she suddenly stopped speaking. They simply strolled back towards the hospital together in an easy silence, until he said with a grin, 'The phone call you made this evening—I hope it was satisfactory.'

She glanced down at her feet, then glanced up at him with a bright smile. 'Oh, yes, fine, thanks.' Katy was over-conscious that she was not strictly speaking the truth, and for a second she thought he might be about to ask more, but he was probably far too polite to do so. She had to remember that the following day they would be working together which made things rather different. More than likely his present charm would evaporate into the inevitable professional attitude of a consultant.

They reached the wicket-gate; he swung it open for her, and she was aware of a tang of fresh cologne about him as she passed through. The strong-featured face, its contours and planes made formidable against the indigo sky, was no longer set and tight-jawed, as it had been in the phone booth earlier. Now a pleasant smile moulded the firm mouth, giving a brief lift to her own spirits, which was quite unexpected.

Their easy conversation had by now reached the rather mundane level of weather patterns in the area, while she moved a little faster to keep pace with his long legs. As they reached the nurses' home, he said, 'Thank you for your company, Sister. I really enjoyed that!'

She paused slightly at the foot of the steps as they exchanged smiles. 'Me too. Goodnight, Mr Hammond. . .'

She ran lightly up the steps, then turned briefly to see him stride away towards the doctors' residential flats. He really seemed quite a nice man, unlike other newcomers, who often arrived full of their own importance, Katy thought as she reached her room, but it was difficult to tell.

As usual, once she was in bed, her subconscious thoughts and anxieties returned to plague her. Warming to someone like Mark Hammond after placing a barrier between herself and any male acquaintance for so long had again brought to the fore the almost unanswerable question: could she trust anyone ever again? Even her work colleagues. . . ?

During her training days at her old London hospital, she had been very naïve. Yet they had been happy times, and although she'd known she possessed a certain youthful innocence it had caused her no problems.

Having passed all her exams, she had been sure that she could never be happier.

It had been on the train when returning to Scotland to help her mother pack for the removal to her present home down south that she had met Steve. She'd happened to be reading a magazine when it had fallen at Steve's feet. He had picked it up with a friendly grin and they had started talking straight away. It had been a whirlwind affair and three months later he had proposed. She'd believed herself at that time to be madly in love; Steve too. Her mother and Ross had been very happy for her, so long as it was what she wanted. Katy had been absolutely confident that she wanted Steve, without a shadow of doubt. . .

Now she stared restlessly past the undrawn curtains. The stars she had gazed at earlier were still shining, only there seemed to be more of them. How well she recalled those heady days when the world had seemed to belong to her and Steve alone. He had owned a small engineering firm in the south of England, which had apparently been doing well, and ultimately he had bought a small house nearby, and she'd begun to apply for jobs in that part of the country.

Following their marriage and the honeymoon, they'd moved into the new house in Basingstoke. The business had been doing well and Steve had had to travel to Europe sometimes for a week or so. He'd rung her almost every day on those occasions. A few months after her marriage, she'd received the first of the anonymous letters—letters which later transpired to be from his legal wife. . .

Wide awake still, Katy got up to make herself some tea. She took it back to bed with her and had a couple of aspirin. One would have imagined that now, two years after her life had been shattered, she might have overcome the sleepless nights and the 'why me?' syndrome.

On the whole she had coped well enough—perhaps too well, for she had cast down all the bitter emotions of such an event rather too deeply into the recesses of her mind. She had learned a great deal since experiencing that sham marriage; it seemed far and away worse than being bereaved of a beloved husband. Such an ugly word as 'bigamy' seemed like a substitute for 'failure'. Hardly a day went by when she did not have to pull herself up sharply, resisting the temptation to believe that she was indeed a failure. She would never forget the loving understanding from her family, Ross particularly. As a solicitor he had been able to help with advice too.

At the hospital she had told no one of her private life, except Miss Munro, who had been kindness itself in her worst moments, particularly when she'd needed time off to attend court for the eventual case against Steve and to hear his subsequent prison sentence, which had been quite short. Ultimately Katy had heard that he had gone to South Africa for good.

But nothing would ever dim the memory of the humiliation she'd endured, the broken pride. Surely such things could never be completely eliminated from anyone's life?

A cool night breeze rustled the curtains suddenly, as unexpectedly a small detail entered her head. Neither she nor Mark Hammond had mentioned their jobs as such, or that they would be working together. They had been talking so much and the conversation had flowed so naturally that she had experienced an unexpected desire to discuss all manner of things with him. Nevertheless she was utterly determined that neither he, nor any other man, would pose a threat to her hard earned peace of mind.

And with such cautious if not optimistic thoughts she fell into a deep sleep.

CHAPTER TWO

IN THE dining room next morning, Katy met Tessa Bailey, her Staff Nurse. 'Hi, Tess!' Katy called as they queued for their eggs and bacon. 'How are things? You're not still worrying about Yvonne, I hope?' Katy thought how pale her friend looked, thick dark hair emphasising the pallor of her skin, brown eyes unsmiling even though she managed a hint of a grin. She knew how seriously Tessa took her work and that she was a born worrier.

They collected their laden trays and found a seat overlooking the grounds. Tessa shook her head. 'No, it's not that, Katy. I'm. . .' She faltered and stopped speaking, beginning to tuck into her food, then she resumed. 'Katy, can I ask you something? I don't mean now—well, later, perhaps, when we have more time?'

In the doctor's section, Katy noticed the tall figure of Mark Hammond stride in, accompanied by Professor Rupert Mason, as she replied, 'Sure, what about tonight? We've both got an ''early'', I believe. I'll check. We could have our dinner, then you could come up to my room. I have some wine and stuff.'

'You're a pal, Katy; thanks a lot!'

'No problem. We'd better get going now, I suppose. Mr Mark Hammond's making his introductory trip to us this morning. I wonder what the real man's like beneath that charm?'

'We'll soon find out!' Tess said soberly as they walked briskly out to Reception and into the lift.

Katy glanced at the watch pinned to her uniform. Good, she had a few minutes in hand to take a brief look around the ward. One never knew who might appear at any time, apart from the illustrious Mark Hammond. She was quite looking forward to seeing his face when he recognised her from last night. If he did, that was!

Fortune was looking its shining best in the morning sunshine, as it happened. While Tess hurried away to supervise breakfast, Katy approved the freshly polished floor, the four-bed units, crisp bright yellow curtains at the windows and a more muted colour in shades of gold and yellow for the bed covers. Flowers were already in place on bedside lockers and tables, and at present they had only one patient, who had given birth the night before and no doubt would be going home that evening if pronounced fit, her empty bed rather suggesting that she was in the bathroom.

With an inner sigh of relief, Katy saw that she might actually have a chance to catch up with her admin if this small lull continued. But it seemed she had thought too soon. . .

'Sister Woods!' One of the young student nurses was calling her from the corridor, and looking decidedly harassed.

'What is it, Nurse?' Katy asked sharply. In her training days they would never have been allowed to hail a senior in that way; they'd jolly well had to deliver a message in the correct textbook manner. Even so, the girl looked quite anxious.

'I went into the office to report that I was on duty, Sister, and Night Sister looked. . .well, very upset. . .' she said, walking towards Katy as if reading her expression.

'Upset?' Katy said, startled. 'OK. You go and give Staff a hand in the kitchen now, would you please? It's breakfast for one on the ward, and two in the private rooms.'

In the office, Night Sister Moura O'Brien looked up from the desk as Katy went in, pushing her night-report book aside. Her dark blue Irish eyes which always held a twinkle of good humour were sad as she said quietly, 'I'm sorry to have to tell you, Katy, but our young patient, Yvonne, was involved in a car accident last night with that fool of a boyfriend of hers. . .' Moura took a deep breath. 'Yvonne, that boyfriend, and the darlin' baby, all dead. . .'

'Oh, no. . .' Katy breathed. 'Oh, I can hardly believe it. Yet I had a feeling something was terribly wrong.'

Moura pursed her lips. 'It seems they were not going to Scotland at all, or to his mother. They were virtually on the run, that's why he was so odd during the birth. Wanted by the police, of course, for a string of house break-ins he'd done here. He thought he could escape up north, taking the girl and baby with him. Mother of God, what a terrible tragedy for them all. . .'

'Did the police get in touch last night?'

'Yes, and I had to break it to Miss Munro this morning. We've all had the same reaction—fury that three young lives should have been wasted so recklessly.'

Katy bit her lip. 'The girl was so happy with her baby, yet the boyfriend obviously dominated her because she left the hospital willingly, it seems.'

Word soon got around the gynae and obs section, causing a wave of sympathy everywhere. Katy was in the intensive care baby unit when Miss Munro entered the ward accompanied by Mr Hammond, both talking quietly, heads down in concentration. Miss Munro glanced up, suddenly seeing Katy.

'Sister, this is Mr Mark Hammond, who will be the new senior consultant gynaecologist and obstetrician in our section. This is Sister Woods, Mr Hammond; she has been with us for the last two years and,' she added with a kindly smile, 'we hope for some time to come yet.'

His handshake was firm and strong. 'Good to meet you. . .formally, Sister,' he said, his smile encompassing her as well as Miss Munro, before he glanced around the unit. 'Not too busy at the moment, I believe?'

'No, the babies we have here are prems; their parents visit each day. I think they will be here for at least another month yet.' His eyes met hers as she spoke, his white cotton coat over an immaculate suit giving him a far more formal air, quite different from when they had strolled along the beach together the night before.

They all walked away from the glass viewing panel and continued into the ward, Mark Hammond having a few pleasant words with the lone patient sitting nursing her child prior to feeding it. Mark Hammond read her notes through, then glanced approvingly at the six-pound baby boy. 'You feel up to going home today, do you, Mrs Hall?'

The woman grinned. 'Oh, yes, Doctor, I'm fine, thank you. Um. . .if I don't see the Professor again, I'd be glad if you would thank him for his kindness to us!'

The consultant gave a broad smile. 'I'll certainly tell him what you said, and all the best to you and your family.'

In the office Miss Munro once again mentioned the sad event of Yvonne Smith's death, before she bustled away leaving Mark Hammond looking interestedly around the neat shelves of files and folders. He glanced at Katy with a grin, a suspicion of a dark shadow on the square chin, teeth a white gleam against the tan he had acquired while working in Brunei. He took down a box file, glancing through the papers it contained. It was labelled 'Patients' Menus.' Nodding, he replaced the box, waving a hand around the room. 'From all of this, I would guess it's your handiwork?'

Katy felt her cheeks go hot; she didn't know if he was laughing at her or not. 'Well, yes, I suppose so, but we all use it.'

'A darned good idea, too.' He perched himself on the corner of the desk, long, slim legs crossed at the ankles, one hand in his trouser pocket, which swept back the white coat, so giving her a glimpse of the belt around his slim waist. The belt had a very unusual buckle in the form of an animal's head, but she could hardly stare at it.

He was saying, 'There may be a few changes I shall want here, Sister, and while we don't seem rushed off our feet I think now is a good time to start.' He glanced up at the office clock, set at twelve midday. 'So, I just have to go downstairs to make a phone call. I'll be back in about half an hour.' He headed for the door, then turned to look at her. 'I wonder why you didn't mention to me last night that we should be working together?'

'The subject didn't seem to crop up,' she said mildly, 'I try to forget work at times.'

He opened the door. 'Yes.' He smiled knowingly. 'Believe it or not, I do understand.'

She stood for a while after he'd gone, wondering what it was about him that made her feel one minute that he was friendly, the next that his words held faint sarcasm. She went over to her desk and sat down, pushing a tendril of soft fair hair behind her ear. Heaven only knew what sort of changes he intended making; she was already too much of an office girl as it was!

Mark Hammond returned on time, looking more withdrawn than when he had been with her earlier; maybe it had something to do with the phone call. He was obviously in a more businesslike mood, and wanted to use her word processor for his new ideas.

'These things are a necessary evil,' he muttered, attacking the keyboard with complete professionalism. 'I have an office downstairs, as you probably know, but I consider it extremely useful to have records of current patients up here.' He grinned, glancing at the screen, while a small cleft appeared to the left side of his mouth. 'So far, the NHS hasn't provided us with a secretary each!' The cheeky grin faded as quickly as it had come. He sat back from the keyboard, saying, 'A bad business about Yvonne Smith and her baby. A shocking waste.'

'Completely,' Katy agreed. 'That beautiful baby, so perfect. . .' Her words trailed off as she thought of her own pointless hopes, as well as of Fleur and Ross and how desperately they wanted a child, which at present seemed to be unlikely to happen for them. 'Life can be very cruel,' she said absently.

Mark agreed with a sigh, noticing the slight quiver of Katy Woods' full pink lips, the sadness in the incredibly blue eyes. Surely it must be due to more than the loss of their patient and the baby? That was shattering enough, but although he hardly knew her he had the instinctive feeling that those eyes revealed far more than she realised, in spite of her rather, at times, coolly efficient demeanour. Or at least that was how it seemed to him.

'Right, Sister,' he said abruptly, running his eyes along the row of box files, 'we're really going to have to reduce some of those, you know.'

A frisson of annoyance went through her. 'I know what you mean, Mr Hammond, but there are more times than not when a member of staff may be scared stiff to use the WP in an emergency. It is far quicker for some of the older part-time nurses to take down a file and give us the information we want.' Her eyes stared into his almost in defiance, her method had worked since this had become her domain and no one had complained thus far.

Mark said, with slight irritation in his tone, 'Yes, I understand fully, Sister, but if I say that some of these people have to move with the times it is not a criticism of you, just a question of making things easier for us all.'

They worked on for the next two hours, until the phone rang and they were informed that three admissions were due on Fortune within the next hour. Katy gave the message to Mark, who looked almost disappointed as he rose to leave. 'Perhaps we can continue this job some other time. Meanwhile I shall have a late lunch and see what Rupert has to say about two things: one, his retirement party in a fortnight's time, and the other, the new registrar he is trying to get to come here and fill one of the vacancies.'

'Do you want me to give you a ring when the three new patients have arrived?'

'No, not unless it's something urgent. I'll be coming in about six this evening to see how things are going.'

He stood up to leave, struck once again as he went through the door by the emptiness in her eyes, which might be coldness, but he didn't think so. Why she intrigued him he had no idea. Perhaps the boyfriend was giving her problems.

He could be quite wrong about her, of course, he thought while waiting for the lift. He was no one to judge such things. Women were an enigma to him. Twice he had imagined himself to be in love and thought faithfulness to be part of it. The first time had been a youthful affair, but the second. . . He pushed the thought away. Janine was thousands of miles from Rosewall, thank heaven, and his step was lighter as he headed for the Prof's office.

Katy spent the rest of the afternoon preparing beds and the labour wards for the incoming patients. One was an antepartum haemorrhage and possible Caesarean, the second a seven-month pregnancy for observation with suspected hypertension, the third an apparently normal beginning of labour, but a first child to a very young mother-to-be of seventeen.

The two first-year students she had on the staff were quite enthusiastic and willing to learn. Nevertheless, it was something of a relief when Tessa arrived back on duty following her time off. 'Things are happening again then?' she said, with a wan smile. 'I thought the lull wouldn't last for long.'

Katy was checking bed linen in the linen room. 'I'm glad you're back, Tess. Could you ring Roger Maynard? I think he's the anaesthetist on duty at the moment; tell him he could be needed tonight. Mr Hammond will confirm when he comes in later.'

It was around six o'clock, just as Katy was planning to go off duty, when Mark arrived; the new patients were by now comfortably settled and anxiously awaiting the doctor's visit.

In the office, Katy handed over the patients' notes which he studied in silence; then he said briskly, 'It looks as if two of them are going to be with us longer than just a couple of nights' stay. The young girl's labour may be straightforward but babies are no respecters of theoretical guidelines.'

She had watched him with intense interest whilst he read the notes; she studied the smooth skin on the good-looking face, assessed the high forehead which more often than not was concealed by a lock of dark hair that refused to stay in one place, the winged brows that protected the deep-set eyes, the imperfect nose with nostrils that flared slightly when a burst of emotion animated his expression. He had well-shaped lips, not too full, that lifted at the corners in laughter but, equally, could become a thin line when his charm of manner was suddenly replaced by a formidable iciness and an iron determination of will. Katy decided she would hate to be on the receiving end of his temper. . .

'I have asked Staff to warn Roger Maynard he may be needed shortly,' she said, averting her eyes from him.

She seemed unable to help herself, it was as if she knew they were on the brink of a very good working relationship or a tempestuous friendship that could threaten her newly acquired calm. It had to be a crazy assumption though, she really must give up all this gazing-into-a-crystal-ball stuff. She still did not know the man, yet something about him was hypnotic, and common sense warned her that she should remember constantly another occasion when it had seemed as if she were slipping over the edge of a precipice and could do nothing about it. . .

Katy pulled her thoughts up sharply, chiding herself for such ramblings when there was work to do. Hurriedly she gathered up the patients' notes and they went into the ward together.

Tessa was with the young seventeen-year-old unmarried mother-to-be. She drew the bed curtains together behind Mr Hammond and Katy, answering the doctor's questions with a calm, pleasant manner. 'Yes, sir, I've completed the physical examination, including examining the abdomen for presentation of lie of foetus.'

'Fine.' Mark Hammond smiled kindly at the young girl. 'Hello, Polly. I have your history notes here from your antenatal visits, and everything seems in order. Now, you've had some pain, earlier this afternoon you had a "show", and since then the rupture of the membranes has occurred. It will probably be a few hours yet before your baby actually arrives, but you're in good hands with us. . .'

'Couldn't it happen any quicker than that?' The girl's large grey eyes filled with tears, her face flushed. 'You see I was hoping my boyfriend, Tim, would come at visiting time tonight and it would all be over.'

Mark Hammond laughed softly. 'My dear, if we could order these babies to arrive at a set time our job here would be a piece of cake!' He turned to Katy as Tessa left them. 'Isn't that right, Sister? We'd be able to organise something like a railway timetable.'

Polly Hanson giggled at Mark's nonsense but it put her at her ease, and Katy could see that the anxious young girl was quite relaxed now and would be looking forward to visiting time.

Tess had arranged that the two younger women would be in the same bay, although the beds were far enough apart for privacy, and Katy pulled the curtains around the bed when they reached Elaine Miller and her husband, Roy. Mark Hammond shook hands with them both, then said with a smile, 'Now, Mrs Miller, how are you feeling?'

She gave a brave imitation of a smile. 'Not too bad thanks, Doctor, it's the pain and the bleeding. . .'

Roy Miller, who had been silent until now, gave Mark a worried look, his shaven head and gold earring emphasising the pallor of his face. He pressed Elaine's hand into his. 'She's worrying about me, Doc, but I'm worrying about her. All I want is for our little baby to arrive safely, then Elaine will be all right—won't you, darlin'?' he said, with a touch of bravado.

Elaine nodded miserably, pain and stress marked on her pretty features. 'I'm going to be OK, Roy, once the baby comes. The doctor's here so there's nothing to worry about.'

Mark Hammond spoke quietly and reassuringly to the couple, explaining that after an examination and further tests he would then be able to decide upon the next course of action.

'I think you and your husband could do with a cup of tea now, Mrs Miller. I'll be back to see you very shortly.' He patted her shoulder comfortingly. 'Everything will be fine, but you must try not to worry. Understood?'

Elaine smiled at this handsome man who looked like a film star. 'Yes, sure, I'll be all right.'

'Good girl. . .'

Mark made some notes, saying to Katy as they crossed the ward to the third patient, 'If I'm not mistaken, Mrs Miller has a moderate bleeding situation. We'll need to set up an intravenous infusion and to monitor the central venous pressure. She'll need fifteen to twenty milligrams of Omnopon to relieve her pain and anxiety, but I'll confirm to the night staff when they come on regarding the findings.'

The next woman was forty-three-year-old Mrs Janet Stacey. Katy introduced her to Mark. 'Hello, Mrs Stacey,' he said. 'Expecting your third baby? We could call you an old hand at the game, then!'

Janet Stacey had a hairdo of short black springy curls, a strong face and dark eyes that looked both wise and very tired. 'Hi, Doctor! Yeah, I thought I'd finished with such things, but you never know your luck, do you?'

'Sister tells me you've been attending the antenatal clinic. Is there any particular reason you know of for this sudden hypertension?'

The woman avoided his eyes, then said in a low voice, 'Oh, just teenage-daughter trouble. She's been playing up—drugs, boys, out all hours. My husband, Pete, and I have been at our wit's end, especially when the police brought her home the other night for joyriding in a stolen car. She's fourteen and still at school—when she thinks she'll turn up. Quite honestly, I'm sure it's school that's ruined her. They get in with a bad lot and there seems to be no turning back. . .'

Mark Hammond nodded. 'Well, you're in here for a rest, Mrs Stacey.' He studied her notes. 'You've been having vaginal bleeding, I believe,' he said easily.

'That's right. Although I feel quite well in myself, considering.'

'Yes, this is often the case. However, we'll be doing an ultrasound scan in the morning so that we can locate the placenta. I mean it—' he grinned, wagging a finger '—when I say you really have to rest, you know; that's why you're in here. Is your husband coming tonight?'

'Yes, I hope so.'

'Good, I'll see him then and tell him what's happening. I'll prescribe a sedative for you, and I want to hear in the morning that you've had a decent night's sleep, OK?'

'Yes, thanks, Doctor.'

Back in the office he wrote out the prescriptions necessary for both women. He handed Katy the form then sat back in his chair, rubbing a hand across his forehead, saying thoughtfully, 'I expect you realised when I did that brief examination of Mrs Miller, her uterus was as hard as wood. She's twenty-eight weeks, and the bleeding is due to placenta abruption or separation of the placenta, of course. Depending on further bleeding, which could be very serious, I'm pretty sure we'll be doing a Caesar tomorrow morning.'

'Yes, I thought that's what it would be,' Katy said, frowning. She looked at him suddenly, as he stretched languidly in the chair. 'Can I order you a tray of tea before you go downstairs?'

'No, thanks, Sister; you were due off duty nearly an hour ago. Staff Nurse Bailey should at this moment be reporting off duty to Night Sister, I hope; otherwise she'll soon be dropping large hints that her staff were here on time so there's no need for day people to be hanging around!'

Katy laughed. 'You seem to know her already, Doctor!'

'Not really, it's just that I know the ropes by now!' He chuckled, thinking it was the first time he had seen Katy Woods laugh as if she meant it. He still wondered. . .

The telephone suddenly buzzed on the desk between them. She picked up the receiver. 'Sister Woods, Fortune Ward.'

A woman's husky voice answered, laced with charm. 'I should like to speak to Mr Hammond, if I may. The receptionist has told me he's available. Thank you so much.'

For some reason, Katy resented the tone of the caller

and said haughtily, 'Just one moment, I'll see if I can contact him.' She placed a hand over the receiver. 'It's for you, Mr Hammond. Female,' she added darkly, but with a twinkle in her eye.

As he took the phone, a small frown creased his brow. 'Hammond here. . . ! Good Lord! What on earth are you doing here. . . ? I thought you were still in Brunei. . . No, I am not off duty until very late this evening. . . Sorry, it just can't be done. . . ! That is entirely your fault, Janine; please do not ring me again at the hospital!'

Katy had gathered up her belongings smartly, not wanting to intrude upon what was obviously a very personal call, but she couldn't help hearing how coldly brusque Mark Hammond was with the woman, whoever she was. Katy had reached the door when Mark slammed down the phone, his face suffused with controlled anger as he stalked past her. He muttered a quick, 'Excuse me,' and strode off towards the lift, calling over his shoulder, 'I'll be back shortly!'

She wished like mad that she had not overheard that conversation; such a thing was always embarrassing. Besides, in a vague sort of way, it made her own rather mawkish meanderings about him look decidedly foolish. He obviously had problems, which made him human like everyone else, instead of the man-of-the-world she had perceived him to be—one who could handle complications of any kind.

Another object lesson for herself, she thought as she made her way downstairs to the dining room, glancing at the collected-post board to see if there was anything for Fortune. There wasn't, and just at that moment Mark Hammond appeared from the office he shared with several other senior medics. She tried to avoid him, thinking he might be disconcerted by her having overheard his phone call. She veered away towards the small corridor that led to the dining room, when to her chagrin she realised he was right behind her in the queue, collecting his meal.

He smiled. 'You don't mind if I join you, do you, Sister?'

What could she say? 'No, of course not. I usually try to get a window seat.'

'Good thinking!' he said. 'Despite my bragging, saying I knew the ropes tonight, I still have a lot to learn!'

Katy thought his dark blue eyes were almost black with tiredness that evening, and she couldn't help feeling a pang of sympathy for him. She said brightly, 'Do you know, when I first came here two years ago they were just building this dining room? It's a wonderful place now, but the chaos then! Being so new and. . .' She nearly said 'and more miserable than I've ever been in the whole of my life', but quickly corrected herself. 'And not knowing a soul, I'd have given anything to be back in my old hospital.' She grinned as they sat down at their table.

He gave a small grimace. 'I know the feeling. In fact, the flat I've been allocated at the doctors' block gives me the same kind of. . .not panic in the true sense, but something rather close to it. I'm afraid I've been rather spoilt with the sort of quarters I've become used to. I know it's difficult with staff changes and so on, but I may seriously think of renting or buying a place here.'

They talked on for a while about local property, the ins and outs of mortgages. Like an ongoing picture reel, the small, attractive house she had lived in with Steve in Basingstoke came to her mind. He had told her that he'd bought it outright, which had turned out to be untrue. How could she have been so naïve as to believe what he'd said without first checking the details? She could only conclude, on looking back, that love really was blind. She pushed the thoughts away quickly, saying, 'I think there's something to be said for doing either. I suppose it rather depends upon people's careers.'

He was gazing at her quizzically. 'Do you mind if we're informal over names off duty?'

'We all do it.' She smiled, pushing the remnants of her trout aside.

'Well, Katy.' He leaned forward slightly, and the close proximity set her heart pounding. Maybe it had something to do with the openness of his expression, the innate kindness, and, of course, the good looks. 'I want to apologise,' he continued, 'for walking out tonight after my phone call. One should never mix business with pleasure, but I'm not going to bore you with it.

'You know, to change the subject, Katy, I've really enjoyed our little chats, but I want you to tell me if I'm encroaching upon your time.' He was uncomfortably aware of the complete hash he was making of explaining his thoughts to this very pleasant girl, who, as far as he was concerned, was just about the most coolly intelligent nurse he had met in Rosewall since his arrival.

Light colour had rushed to her cheeks at his compliment. She was saying, 'Well, as a matter of fact, I do have an appointment with a friend this evening.' She noticed the slight embarrassment on his features, or could it have been irritation? Either way she could not let Tess down by being late. 'I really have to go now, I'm afraid. . . See you tomorrow.'

As she left he rose politely from his chair, then he sat and finished his meal. Before returning to the ward, he intended telling the receptionist that he wanted no calls whatsoever put through to his flat unless medically absolutely necessary. He caught a glimpse of Katy walking across the lawns, her tall, slender figure elegant to watch as she entered the nurses' residence. He pondered again upon what it was that intrigued him about her, despite the thunderclouds of his private life which seemed already to be gathering about him yet again.

He also decided he wanted few outside calls to the hospital either!

Katy undressed, showered and got into her dressing gown. She was just setting out the wineglasses when Tessa tapped at her door. Katy opened it, to find Tessa dressed in much the same apparel as herself. It seemed to be an unwritten rule between them all when on late duty to be comfortable and informal. 'Hi, Tess. Come in and sit down. You look about as appealing as I do!' Katy teased, her long hair falling forward as she put the glasses down on the small coffee-table.

'Yeah, I sometimes wonder why we do this job. And yet, do you know, when I have my days off, I seem to think of nothing but all of us back here? Well, until a couple of weeks ago, that is. . .'

They settled in comfortable chairs, and Katy pushed some nibbles across the table. 'Help yourself, Tess.' She glanced up at her friend. 'There's nothing wrong is there? Really wrong, I mean?'

'Well, I suppose there is and there isn't.'

'Oh, come on, Tess, you had better start from the beginning!'

Tess gave a large sigh and stared into her glass. 'Well, you remember back in the spring when I told you Roger Maynard—you know, one of the anaesthetists—gave me a lift home from Chelmsford?'

'Yes, I remember. What about him?'

'We've been seeing each other from time to time. Going out occasionally for a drink, driving to places of interest through the summer, all that stuff, and, well. . .' Tess ran her hands over her face. 'I don't quite know how to tell you this.'

Katy sipped her wine thoughtfully. 'Hang on, Tess, there's nothing wrong in going out with this character, is there? He's quite good-looking, except that I don't go much for blond men, but that's neither here nor there. . .'

Tess was shaking her head. 'Katy, for God's sake, tell me you won't breathe a word to anyone about this. I ought to know better at twenty-nine, but I just don't seem able to help myself. . .'

'What is it, then, Tess? Has he turned out to be a rogue or something?'

'Actually, he's too nice if that's possible. He really is great, Katy.' Her dark eyes lit up with a fleeting happiness which just as quickly disappeared. 'We seem to have so much in common: we both have the same sense of humour, love tennis, hate swimming, love the theatre, books and plays. . .'

'Has he. . . ?'

'If you mean, have we slept together—yes.' Tess answered quickly as if she might change her mind. 'That's part of the trouble. We'd been out one evening, had a meal, went to the theatre at Colchester, it was all so. . .so right. Then we went back to his flat—he rents a place just the other side of Maldon, to be reasonably close to the hospital. Well, you can guess what happened. He says he loves me. I certainly love him; I've never felt like this about anyone before. It's. . .just perfect. If we meet at work, even the dullest job has a glow about it when I'm near him, and I'm sure he feels the same about me.'

'Hasn't he told you, then?'

'Yes, sort of,' Tess said, lips quivering, 'but last night he came out with the fact that he's married. It happened five years ago. The first year apparently was fine, then his wife's health began to deteriorate, and subsequently she was found to be suffering from MD. Roger bought them a bungalow, all fitted up so that she can get around as normally as possible.

'Even worse, Katy, she was in a wheelchair when he took me in to meet her; she had told him to bring his friends home, and he agreed, thinking someone on the staff who worked with him would cheer her up. I wish to God I hadn't gone. She's such a sweet, happy person. Helen's her name; she's so pretty, copper curls, beautiful skin. . .and—well, she's not getting better and may soon have to spend more of her time in an iron lung; you know what muscular dystrophy's like. . .'

Tears sprang again to Tess's eyes, and her voice shook. 'She wants me to visit her whenever I can, which I promised to do. Roger told me that sex is impossible between them. I know he hates himself for what he's doing, but he loves me. . .and says this is all he has to offer. I'm at my wit's end, Katy. I just don't know what to do.' Her lips trembled as she buried her face in her hands. 'I'm so sorry I'm like this, but everything seems so impossible. Yet I'm crazy about Roger, and when we're together. . .neither of us can think of anything else but the next time. . .'

She looked up at Katy in despair. 'I know I'm making it sound as if the sex is the only thing. It isn't; we simply love being in each other's company. . .'

Katy stood up and crossed quickly to her friend's chair, kneeling and putting an arm around Tess's shaking shoulders. 'Oh gosh, I had no idea you were going through all this. Why didn't you tell me before? It's one hell of a state to be in. At this moment, Tess, love, I can't think of any immediate help, except that you know you can come to me at any time and we can always talk things through.'

Tessa mopped her tears, smiling bravely. 'That's all I was hoping you'd say, Katy; you'll never know how much it means to me. How can I mention it to anyone else? Roger is so understanding; he's even saying he would not blame me if I just upped and left him. But I can't, Katy. Poor chap, he's only thirty-three, with this terrible weight of worry about Helen on his mind, as well as the guilt. But I can't possibly contemplate leaving him; my hell is nothing to his. How I wish I'd met him years ago. . .'

She blew her nose, looking slightly less desperate. 'But please, Katy, don't drop any kind of hint that you know a thing. I don't want him to lose his job over me; these days one can't be too careful. He loves Helen dearly and couldn't possibly leave her; I wouldn't want him to, of course. But oh, Katy, it's so hard. . . Sorry.' She sniffed. 'I'll be OK in the morning; I feel better now that you know and I can talk about it.'

'Are you really sure you'll be OK, Tess?'

'Yes, thanks. It's surprising how people can put on a brave face each day under difficult circumstances, isn't it? We should be the ones to know!'

Katy smiled wryly. Tessa had no idea how relevant the words were to her own situation. 'Tess, now listen—what about you and me going into the town tomorrow evening and dropping in at the winebar there?'

'That would be great, Katy. Are you sure you can spare the time?'

'Quite sure.' Katy smiled, and Tessa went off to her room. She gave a small grin to herself as she collected up the glasses. That was the second time today she had been asked if she could spare the time. What people didn't realise was that, apart from her work, it was a sad fact that she had all the time in the world.

CHAPTER THREE

ON FORTUNE WARD next morning there was an air of urgency. Night Sister O'Brien had reported that Mrs Miller had awakened in the night from a deep sleep in great pain. Mr Hammond had been sent for at six a.m., and was returning soon, having made the decision to operate.

'I've reported to Theatre Sister,' Moura told Katy. 'I'll leave you now to proceed with the pre-prep. Mr and Mrs Miller have had the reason for a Caesarean explained to them; permission has been given and signed for. The patient's past obstetric and medical history has been recorded, and I think that's nearly it. . .'

'A check's been made that cross-matched blood's available?' Katy said.

'Oh, yes, although most departments now reserve two units of E rhesus negative blood for labour usage, don't they? Thank heaven.' Moura picked up her bags. 'I've alerted the anaesthetist, and peds man. I'm not quite sure who we'll be getting yet, but they're standing by, anyway.

'Mrs Miller was given sodium citrate orally about a half an hour ago. That still leaves time for the pre-prep, the pre-med injection and Mr Hammond's lovely voice with soothing words!' She glanced at the desk. 'It's all in the report book. Anyway, my darlin', I'm off now; I'm dead beat!'

'OK. Thanks a lot, Moura. Sleep tight!'

Katy had already given Mrs Miller her pre-med by the time Mark Hammond strode into the ward to her bedside, giving Katy a brief nod and a, 'Good-morning, Sister.'

He smiled at Elaine Miller. 'Hi there, Mrs Miller; we're all set, then?'

'Yes.' Elaine smiled drowsily. 'I don't care what happens now as long as the baby's OK.'

'That's the spirit!' He grinned. 'You'll be fine, I promise you.' He glanced behind him. 'I see your husband's arrived, so I'll send him along to you. See you later, Mrs Miller.'

Katy squeezed the girl's hand. 'The porter will be here in a minute to take you to the theatre; Staff Bailey will be with you, and I'll be there shortly.'

Elaine's husband met her at the door of the ward. 'She will be OK, won't she, Sister?' His eyes were heavy with lack of sleep and anxiety.

'Yes. Go along and see her now, Mr Miller. You can stay with her until we get to the ante-theatre. Don't worry; she's in very good hands, I can assure you.'

Once Katy had checked that Elaine's notes were with her; Tessa arrived, and the group set off for the theatre. Katy instructed the two first-years to prepare a post-op bed, before hurrying to join the others. Roy was holding his wife's hand, then bent to kiss her forehead gently before the theatre doors closed upon him.

In the ante-theatre Mark had already been gowned and masked by Theatre Sister; Roger Maynard, the anaesthetist, checked that his patient was fully unconscious, then he gave the go-ahead to Mark. As a senior midwife, Katy would be at his side until the paediatrician arrived, in case the foetus lost blood and needed urgent resuscitation, but they were not at that stage just yet. Katy noticed the calm and able way that Mark was assessing the swollen abdomen before making the final confirmation of a Caesarean.

Mark muttered whilst he further examined the patient. 'The placenta is spongy. Brisk bleeding indicates the need for immediate delivery, in this case a Caesar as we are now getting severe bleeding.'

He glanced up at the group around the table in the main theatre. 'Ladies and gentlemen, we are about to perform a Transverse Pfannenstiel's incision, which you know is cosmetically pleasing.' He held the scalpel poised, then skilfully proceeded to make the horizontal cut. 'This method,' he murmured, for the benefit of two young trainee housemen behind the viewing screen, while moving slightly to allow Theatre Sister to use the swabs, 'is less painful and gives better post-operative mobility for the patient.'

It seemed hot in the theatre beneath the lights, and the scrub nurse passed dry gauze to Sister for her to mop Mark Hammond's brow. Everyone was tense at this point, knowing that this particular operation could only be carried out by a skilled and experienced surgeon. A silence ensued as he worked. The foetal head was now revealed, and the delivery was facilitated with a free hand.

Katy moved forward to clear the airways, allowing time for the baby's shoulders to be delivered. The cord was clamped and cut. The placenta was removed manually and the uterine cavity checked to ensure emptiness.

Mark looked at the newborn boy child. Katy removed it from the mother while the closing of the wound began. Somewhere outside a telephone could be heard. No one dared to move, until at last the persistent noise penetrated Mark's concentration on the delicate suturing.

'For God's sake, someone go and strangle that crazy receptionist for putting a call through to us! She's seen the ops timetable, hasn't she?' he snapped, skilful fingers still working.

Katy handed the child to the paediatrician, who had just entered and was waiting for his part of the job, carrying out the checks. He indicated to Katy with raised eyebrows that she was able to leave. Once through the doors of the theatre she threw off her sterile clothing, washed her hands, smoothed down her uniform and hurried downstairs to Reception.

Margaret, the girl at the switchboard who had been with them barely three months, gasped with what seemed to be relief when Katy appeared. 'Oh, Sister, thank heaven you've come! I know I shouldn't have rung the theatre, but it's this woman on the phone again who is pleading to see Mr Hammond. She's quite nice, really, but I think there might be something wrong, and I feel rather sorry for her!'

Katy was sorry for Margaret. 'Didn't you tell her he might call back later if it's urgent?'

'Yes. . .' The outside phone rang again. 'That's her now, I bet.'

'I have to get back to the theatre, Margaret. Just tell the woman he is not available. If she wants to take a taxi and wait here, that's up to her, but don't tell her I said so.'

Katy hurried back to the theatre. Elaine Miller was just being brought out to the ante-theatre, still unconscious. Tessa was there, assessing breathing, pulse, blood pressure and the general state of the patient. 'So far, so good. . .' Tessa murmured, glancing sideways as Roger Maynard busied himself with washing and changing, giving her a tired smile.

Katy noticed, but carried on as if nothing had happened, and yet she almost sensed the emotional tension between the two. She answered Tessa, with approval of the reliable way she always dealt with her work. 'These vital signs are certainly important with such a case as Elaine's, Tess. There's been so much bleeding. We'll have to watch that from the wound, of course, particularly with antepartum haemorrhage. She needs to be kept comfortable later with analgesics, and the temp to be taken regularly, et cetera.'

Katy was talking mainly for the benefit of the young first-year nurse with her. Melanie still looked as if she was really interested in what was going on, and as yet showed far more intelligence than Sandra.

At that moment Mark Hammond chose to appear, throwing off his 'greens' to bare his tanned torso, and Katy all but blinked when he sluiced his hands and forearms at the washbasin, and Tessa, Melanie in tow, gently moved the still unconscious patient to the recovery room.

Mark was halfway to the small shower for male doctors only when he suddenly stopped in his tracks, saying to Katy, 'Did you sort out that problem with Elaine's husband, reassuring him that he could sleep here during the daytime in one of the available rooms?'

'Yes, I did; he certainly seemed to appreciate it. When he goes off to work tonight I'm sure it will be better for him. He needed some persuading, though!'

'I bet. Poor devil.'

Katy returned to the ward just in time to say farewell to young Polly Hanson, whose baby had been born the night before with consummate ease. Tim, her boyfriend, had come to collect her. He could not have been much older than Polly, but apparently both sets of parents were supporting them through their new problems and their ongoing education. 'Bye, then, Sister; thank you for everything; you've been very kind.'

'Goodbye, Polly! Lots of luck to you!'

Katy carried the newborn child out to the taxi, and placed it gently into Polly's arms. As they drove away, Katy gave a small sigh of relief, thinking how nice it was to hear of families drawing together in time of trouble rather than of the splintering of groups that so often happened when a crisis emerged.

Back on the ward she was glad she had an evening off, and was looking forward to going out with Tess; it would be quite a change for. . .

She looked up suddenly from her desk. Mark had flung the office door open, his face taut and angry; then he ran a hand over his chin as if he could somehow clear the expression away, but it wasn't possible as he burst out, 'Why in heaven's name, Katy, didn't you tell me that our nuisance phone call this morning was for me?'

Katy felt her hackles rise at his accusatory tone. 'For the simple reason that you were not in a situation to enable you to take it!'

'Granted, but the first time I hear about it is from this. . .this. . .acquaintance of mine who has been sitting downstairs insisting upon seeing me!'

'That's what I thought you wanted when she rang last time. You gave instructions she was not to ring you here. That's how I understood it, anyway.'

'And you were right, but at least I must know what's going on! I had no idea she would be sitting down there, and, believe me, I do not want too many shocks like that! It was bad enough on my first night here; she had managed to find out where I was and reach me on the phone.'

He slumped down into a chair, his long body stretched dejectedly. 'Sorry about this, Katy; I shouldn't burden you with my private worries, but all I ask is that you keep me informed if it happens again. It's a wretched situation. After practically threatening her to keep her away from here, I bundled Janine into a taxi and got a promise of sorts from her not to come again, but I have my doubts as to how long it will last. . .' He gave a huge sigh.

'I'm so damned tired tonight, forgive me for coming to you just as you're going off duty. . .' He stood up suddenly, giving a sad little smile, his eyes crinkling attractively at the outer corners. 'Please forget it ever happened, and I promise there will not be a repeat performance!'

Katy smiled, quite ready to do as he asked. 'I understand, Mark. We all have our problems, and none of us deal with them in the same way. Life can be a devil, I know that.'

He looked more at ease. 'I always knew I'd have a friend in you, Katy Woods. Goodnight, then, for now.' His eyes held hers briefly, then with the back of his hand he gently brushed the side of her cheek, and he was gone.

That evening, Katy was almost inclined to talk to Tessa about the episode while they enjoyed their visit to the wine bar, but decided that perhaps reticence was best. The bar was none too crowded, and they could actually hear themselves talk. Tessa was not so tense. Suddenly, she said, 'Katy, you've really made me feel so much better since our talk together, but I don't want you to think that each time we meet like this I'm going to start droning on about my troubles over Roger.'

'Of course not, Tess. I meant what I said about us getting together any time. Actually I've had one or two thoughts on what we discussed, and my feelings are that you could continue to carry on discreetly seeing Roger whenever possible, visit Helen, and somehow try to do a sort of balancing act—for now anyway. It's obviously going to become a part of life for you, and at the moment keeping Helen happy is the main thing. Then Roger and you can take whatever is left. After that it will have to be in the lap of the gods.'

Tess looked almost radiant. 'Oh, Katy, I'd been thinking along those lines myself. And yet—' her eyes became sad again '—it seems so selfish on my part.'

Katy shrugged. 'There's only one other way, Tess, and only you can make that decision. . .'

They talked on for a while, and then moved to less serious topics. 'Hey—' Tess grinned '—what are you going to wear at the Prof's retirement party?'

'Well, I thought of buying something; it's ages since I have,' Katy admitted ruefully. It was ages since she'd had any interest in clothes. The last two years seemed to have driven such things out of her head, one way and another.

'In that case, so will I!' Tess said brightly. 'Let's make it our next day off. . .' Her face dropped. 'Oh, we can't have the same day off, can we? Oh, heck, I'd have really liked that. . .'

Katy laughed. 'No need to look so glum; I can probably get the same afternoon off as you with a bit of switching around. Then so long as we only shop locally we'll have four hours to spend our lovely money!'

'Right! Next week it is, then!'

They had a final drink, and by the time they finished the church clock had struck eleven. It was a cool, clear evening with quite a few people about, and as the two girls walked towards the bus stop Tess suddenly tugged at Katy's arm.

'Hey, look, over there, coming out of the hotel. Isn't that Mark Hammond with a woman? Perhaps it's the one who made him hopping mad when you had to leave the theatre for the phone.'

'I don't know,' Katy said, glancing at the expensively dressed woman, who was tall, slender, evidently in a happy frame of mind and smiling up into Mark Hammond's face. It was difficult to see his, for at that moment he and the woman veered off into the car park. 'I definitely didn't get the impression from what Margaret told me that the two of them were all that close. Still, he's a very attractive man; there's probably a whole string of women waiting to catch up with him.'

'Well, he's not going to do much work if he takes them all out to dinner one by one, in that case!'

Katy laughed at Tess's remark as they boarded the bus. Just then Mark's car overtook the bus, and from her window seat Katy saw them chatting easily. Mark Hammond no longer showed the disapproval on his face that had been so noticeable a few hours before.

Lying in bed that night, going over the events of

the last few hours, Katy could not deny that she had experienced a faint stab of disappointment over Mark Hammond and his private life. But, there again, after her own experience why should she be disappointed? She had endeavoured to convince herself since she had been at Rosewall that most men were philanderers, and Mark Hammond was probably no exception.

A week later, Katy was having breakfast with Joanna, her friend from A and E. They had been discussing the Professor's retirement party, and Joanna had hooted with laughter, saying, 'And what do you think? Ron Green imagines he's taking me!'

'You mean he's asked you?'

'No, he says he's *taking* me! He's got a nerve! I told him I'd already made my arrangements. I haven't, of course, but what a cheek!'

'Well, you have to give him full marks for trying. So what will you do?'

'I'll leave it as long as possible, then if I'm desperate I may give in!'

Katy grinned. 'Better than nothing! He might be quite different when you know him socially.'

'Hmph. . . Anyhow, what about the luscious Mark Hammond? I've heard one or two tales about a woman hounding him, but I think they make it up on the grapevine as they go along. I haven't seen much of him.'

'Not surprising. A few days ago we had six admittances *all* on the same day. We were madly busy, but thank heaven those deliveries were normal. Mark Hammond really has been rushed off his feet, but we should be getting another registrar quite soon. We still have a patient who had a Caesar last week, but she's doing OK now. Six like that would have been a nightmare!'

Joanna's eyebrows shot almost up to her brown curls. 'Hell's bells. What a thought!'

'To return to Ron Green for a minute, have you heard any more of his thoughts on the great outside world lately?'

'No, I'm not interested in his deliberations, Katy. I've been so busy myself on A and E, and that army sister's enough for me to cope with when she's on duty. Before I forget, how's Fleur? She's had her mastectomy, I gather.'

'Yes, four days ago, so she's over the worst. I hope to get a weekend off soon to go and see her.'

'That's great! Give her my best when you do. If Fleur gets over this as well as my sister-in-law did, she'll be running around like nobody's business in a few weeks.'

Katy smiled. 'Let's hope so, Jo. I'll give her your message anyway. I'll be dropping in at A and E later for a sub towards the Prof's present, so don't spend everything on a new dress.'

'As if I would!' Joanna grinned as they parted company.

Katy went to phone her mother and then hurried upstairs to Fortune. Her mother had sounded much brighter, and in a day or two when Ross arrived Fleur's progress might be even better. Katy headed for her office, not looking where she was going, her mind on other things. . .and found herself steadied in Mark Hammond's arms, his dark blue eyes laughing down into hers. 'Nice habit, Sister, you and I colliding—for the second time, I believe. A bit early in the day for it, though, wouldn't you say?'

Katy's heart was beating madly. Not only did she feel an idiot but she realised she was not set free as quickly as the time before. Deftly she moved to one side and his arms fell from her. 'I'm sorry—'

He broke in. 'Don't tell me, I know—you've been on the telephone!' The brief contact with her supple curves had set up an old familiar feeling that he had not been troubled with for a very long time. At thirty-eight one was selective.

Her eyes of such incredible blue laughed up at him. 'As a matter of fact I have,' she admitted boldly.

'That boyfriend of yours is a very lucky man!'

She grinned noncommittally, turning towards the office. 'I must go. Night Sister will be blaming me for keeping her from her bed!'

'Then she'll have to do the same for me, because that's why I'm up here at this time of morning. I've taken my regular jog—hence the outfit—and thought I'd put you ladies in the picture.' He stretched a hand out to the door in front of him. 'After you, Sister. . .'

Moura looked up suddenly when she saw them together. 'Honest to God, to what do I owe this small invasion?'

Mark grinned, glancing at Katy. 'If I may just inform you both, it looks as if I'm going to get the new registrar I wanted. He starts today, and I'll be bringing him along with me on my first round later this morning.'

Moura looked stunned. She could afford to, having been a stalwart on the staff at Rosewall for some twenty years. 'Well, Doctor, I'm most impressed! That's the first time I've ever known our head man to tell us such news in advance. How very nice!'

Katy could see that Moura was lapping up Mark's charm, but Moura had plenty too—so much so that it was a further quarter of an hour before Katy was left alone to read the night report and get the rest of her nurses in her office to put them in the picture.

'Everything has been relatively quiet during the night, Nurses. The Intensive Care babies are still increasing their birth weight, the paediatrician will be in this morning for his usual check-up and—' she smiled at Melanie '—I'd like you to be in attendance while he's there. If it's your intention to become a midwife you can pick up quite a lot from these sessions.'

'Thank you, Sister,' Melanie said brightly.

'Mrs Miller must continue her physiotherapy and getting up for a short while, always provided there is no hypertension. Staff Nurse Bailey will check that if I'm not here. Mrs Stacey is improving—the vaginal bleeding has been reduced—and Mr Hammond was saying yesterday she may be able to go home for the weekend, still resting, but back here for another two weeks or so. We want to make sure her baby has as smooth a birth as possible. Right, Nurses, off you go now. I'll be in the kitchen helping with breakfasts in just a few minutes.'

While Katy had been talking, she had glanced out of the window, thinking what a perfect morning it was, and had been surprised to see the woman whom she had seen with Mark Hammond walking through the grounds. She stood up; now there was no sign of her. If, of course, it had been the same person. There were always plenty of people about the hospital at this time of day. Maybe it was just coincidence and someone else rather uncannily resembled the woman. . .

The phone broke into her reverie just then. It was Mark, sounding rather curt. 'Sister, I am most sorry, but I'm afraid I must delay the round for about a half hour or so. I cannot say more at this stage.'

Katy replaced the receiver. How odd, after his making such great play of the introductions to be made that morning. Could she still be right with regard to the companion he'd had with him? Nevertheless, there was no time now to dwell upon it.

'Do you think I'll be able to go home at the weekend, Sister Woods?' Janet Stacey was asking now that breakfast was over in the ward.

Katy noticed how pale and worried she looked. Despite the gradual improvement in the woman's condition recently, she was convinced that Janet's family life was troubling her badly. She said cautiously, 'Well, Mr Hammond only suggested there might be a possibility, Janet; I think I must leave it to him when he comes in later on. Can I help in any way? It's not your daughter again, is it?'

Janet nodded, giving a big sigh. 'I'm afraid it is. When Pete talked to me last night, I knew she was playing up.'

'Playing up?' Katy queried.

'Yes. You see, since I've been away she's been driving Pete nearly round the bend—asking for money he hasn't got, threatening to leave home to go to London and get a job instead of finishing properly at school. I just know she's taking advantage with me not being there. She's been in here to see me with her dad, and of course butter wouldn't melt in her mouth then; she can twist him so easily around her little finger, and he gives in for a quiet life.

'Funny, though, I have an idea she's like this because I'm in here and there's the possibility of a new little one. You see, the other two are boys; she's always been special really, particularly to Pete—he'd give her the moon if he could. Now since I've been in here and had time to think I realise this could be the problem.'

'I think you're not far wrong, Janet. Look, we don't want you having a set-back and losing that baby. In fact in my opinion, seeing that I know the problem, I don't think you should go home and get all worked up about things. Look, why not have a talk to Pete, and see if in his heart he feels the same way as you about your daughter? I have a feeling that once the new baby arrives, which isn't more than a few weeks away now, if you get your girl to look after Peter, make her feel grown-up and part of the arrangements for the arrival of the new baby, things might change—not all at once of course, but it could work.'

Janet Stacey's face looked pensive. 'You know, you could be right, Sister. We've only really had trouble since I told her I was having the baby; it just got worse from then on.'

'Well, now, let's see how we go. The first thing is to get Pete to see things from your point of view.'

When Mark Hammond arrived later, he was accompanied by Professor Mason and William Lodge, the new registrar. A studious-looking man, possibly in his early forties, with dark, thinning hair, he had a stocky figure of medium height and intelligent brown eyes that seemed to smile out upon the world with a benign calm that probably few had and many would aspire to. He was known to his colleagues as Bill Lodge, and Katy took to him immediately.

Introductions were made all round, niceties exchanged, then followed a tour of the ward, after which Katy ordered coffee for all in the office.

'You run a good ship here, Sister,' Bill Lodge remarked with an approving grin, eyes twinkling behind his horn-rimmed specs.

'Thank you, Doctor!' She smiled, pleased at the compliment. 'The staff are tremendous, busy or not, and we certainly have a few rough seas at times!'

'Ah! You don't happen to be a weekend sailor like me by any chance, I suppose?'

'As a matter of fact my father was in the Royal Navy for many years, so the sea is second nature to me. Although I haven't done much recently, sailing is one of my hobbies I don't think I'll ever tire of.'

Mark Hammond, who until now had been happy to allow the others to do most of the talking, was looking somewhat introspective, if not detached, while Rupert Mason went on to extol the virtues of the new section he had helped to plan and was his pride and joy. Now the senior consultant seemed to remember where he was, saying suddenly, 'Well, Bill, you must have realised by now you've certainly hit the right nautical note here, where sailing ships were coming into Maldon long before we were even thought of. Isn't that so, Professor?'

'Absolutely.' Professor Mason beamed, launching into the story of the tea clipper *Fortune*, and the resultant business down the years that had ultimately led to this present section of Rosewall.

Conversation flowed, until the Professor had to leave for an appointment, and Bill Lodge and Mark went off to the wing where the private rooms were situated, which, apart from emergencies, were run by a separate group of nurses.

That afternoon Katy was helping Elaine Miller to feed her new baby, explaining to her how to lie full length on her bed, resting the child on a soft pillow at her side.

'Oh, this is much better, Sister.' She smiled, settling comfortably.

'It's certainly the best position while your abdominal wound is still tender. . .' Katy could hear the telephone ringing. 'I'll leave you now, Elaine; the baby's quite comfortable. At the end of the feed, remove him from the nipple by pressing on his chin, or putting your finger between his lips, and that'll release the vacuum.'

In her office, Katy answered the phone. 'Fortune Ward. Sister Woods here.'

'Mark Hammond here, Katy. Forgive the informality on duty, but I'm in desperate need to talk. Is that possible this evening?'

'Um. . .about work?'

'No, that's the point. It's a private matter and I really would like to talk something over with you. That is, if you had not planned anything else this evening?'

'Well, no.' Her heart was beating ridiculously fast. Was she involved in any way? Was it to do with the woman he'd said was hounding him? Difficult to know, and in her mind was the recollection of him with a woman leaving the hotel and showing no particular signs of anxiety. She kept it low-key, saying, 'I'm due off duty at five this evening; shall we meet in the senior common room? I could have dinner after I've seen you.'

There was a slight pause, then he said quietly, 'I was thinking of getting away from here. Maybe drive out to the country; there's plenty of it around here! Perhaps have dinner together. . .?'

'Well. . . I. . .' Was she being wise or foolish to agree to his suggestion?

The small silence prompted him to say, 'Katy, please don't think there are any ties in this. You know that I have high regard for your integrity; I just want some advice from your angle. I mean, your boyfriend couldn't object to that, surely?'

His assumption that there was a boyfriend in the background was not a bad thing. She thought quickly. If he really did want to talk, then apart from the woman who was obviously troubling him he appeared not to have too many contacts, as one didn't when arriving home from a long spell abroad. 'OK, what time do you think?'

'Will seven o'clock be OK?'

'Sure, fine.'

'Right, I'll pick you up at the nurses' home entrance.'

When she replaced the receiver, Katy realised that her hand was trembling slightly. It irritated her, and yet she knew his request had caused a certain frisson of excitement deep down within. After all, he was asking for her help, and it seemed that the woman in his life was something of a thorn in his side.

In a strange sort of way she could feel quite safe now regarding her fluctuating emotions in his presence. Her own invulnerability to men, so painfully built up, could withstand Mark Hammond's attraction for her with no chance of it showing. She still didn't understand the suddenness of it after two years of having no interest whatsoever in the opposite sex. Sceptics would say that

that was the very reason she had been drawn to him, but she knew better.

The fact also that she had, according to him, a boy-friend was a further guard that would not be difficult to keep up, and she had no intention of letting that guard slip. . .

She remembered Steve the first night she'd gone out with him—the charm, the honeyed words, the promises that had fallen to dust after she'd received at least six letters after the first one from his legal wife while he'd been in Europe. Katy could see his face to this day, the smiling, easy manner, hear the deep, mellifluous voice, the protestations of love till the end of time. It had meant nothing. Not that every other man should be blackened by such behaviour, but Katy had learned a great deal that would wrap her in a safety net against any further dangers of the sort she might encounter. And with a deep sigh she turned and tidied her desk, her thoughts immediately upon work.

After a busy afternoon on the ward, as well as a question-and-answer session for an hour with the two young first-year nurses, she eventually crossed the hospital grounds, unable to help noticing a black, threat-ening sky that was obviously going to preclude a fine evening. A strong wind fluttered her cape outwards as she was buffeted along. She knew that the coastal weather patterns in this area could so often indicate a bad spell for a week or two, which seemed to imply that summer was officially over and autumn had quite definitely arrived.

Once at the nurses' home entrance, she quickly sprinted up the stone steps and headed for her room to get changed.

CHAPTER FOUR

THE Old Barge Inn, to which Mark Hammond took Katy to dinner, was quaint indeed. The hostelry was in fact the solid, sturdy hull of a venerable sailing barge that had plied its cargo up and down the east coast of Britain until such vessels had outgrown their usefulness in a changing world. The old barge was now safely beached, and had been purchased by an enterprising group of caterers who provided the sort of cuisine that people came for from miles around. Even the threatening clouds now seemed to have cleared into a fine evening.

Katy gasped after they had parked the car and walked along the firm gangplank with its white rope rail. 'This is fantastic, Mark! I've never been here but I've heard a lot about it.'

'There you are, you see; I did my homework and decided this would be just right for us. I'm told the food's good, there's soft music, mellow lighting and no hassle!'

She laughed as they stepped aboard, eagerly admiring the ceilings of mahogany tastefully draped with large, wide-gauge fishing nets; its white walls were hung with nautical lamps, anchors and old prints of ships in full sail.

They were shown to the dining room on the spacious lower deck, its old oak beam ends, which supported the decks and joined the sides, wound decoratively with stout hemp rope.

'Looking for all the world like a larger version of first-class saloon in a luxurious yacht!' Mark laughed as he took the menus from the waiter while he and Katy settled at one of the widely spaced tables with chairs cushioned in royal blue linen edged with white piping.

Katy was impressed with their situation at the far end of the dining room, where the view through a large brass-edged porthole alongside the table enabled them to see the broad, snake-like curves of the river as it flowed out to the estuary.

'Have you decided what you're having to eat, Katy?' Mark asked with a smile, at the same time admiring the smooth honey tan of her profile.

Quickly she withdrew her eyes from the wide vista of blue and white sky, streaked now with a flush of gold to the west. 'Sorry, Mark, there's so much to look at as well as the menu! Yes, I've made up my mind, thanks.'

Both chose lobster Thermidor served with a green salad, enhanced by a Californian wine of Mark's recommendation. 'I hope you like it,' he said as the waiter poured and left them. 'I have a very good friend whom I worked with in San Francisco on a six month course of study I did at one of their hospitals there. We've kept in touch ever since, and periodically he has a case of the stuff sent to me!'

'How nice.'

He watched her tilt the glass to her lips, and thought again how attractive she was, but for the constant sadness in her eyes.

'Terrific!' she told him, with an almost childish delight in the wine and the surroundings, as if she had not experienced such small pleasures for a long time. And he wondered whether or not he should embark upon what he wanted to say to her or postpone it, but somehow the conversation went its own way while they enjoyed the delicious food and talked about Maldon and the surrounding countryside.

Katy gave Mark up-to-date news about the much discussed marina, and the age it had taken to build in the face of local opposition. Books, music and theatre later seemed to lead them into further avenues of interest, and it did not seem very long before both realised that a tray of fragrant coffee had been set down before them.

Mark was looking pensive as he poured her a cup and handed it to her. 'I don't quite know what my parents would have thought of the changes here. . .'

She looked at him quickly. 'Your parents are not. . . ?'

'Dead? Oh, no, thank heaven! They moved to Cornwall a few years back when my father retired. So long as he's near the sea he's happy! My mother too—she just revels in it; trouble is, she's always wanting me to drive down there. But lately. . .well, not everything I do is fully approved of.'

Katy grinned. 'That's parents for you!' While talking, her gaze had been drawn down river to the sun-baked mud flats, where thick tufts of sea grass, clumps of wild celery, and sea-asters shone, gilded by the setting sun, along with tarred rope and, incongruously, an old kettle festooned with seaweed. 'Isn't this a fantastic place, Mark?' Katy said suddenly, looking back at him. 'I've never before had the chance to see the estuary this way. I've promised myself so many times that I'd get onto the water, taking a small boat perhaps when the river was just at the right level. Trouble being, when it is, you can bet I'll not be available!'

He chuckled. 'You know, Katy, it's great talking to someone of like mind. I—' He broke off suddenly, his expression changing. 'But I must stop this kind of talk now, I mustn't take up your time unnecessarily. . .' He gazed into her lustrous eyes that even now seemed to have absorbed so much for one so young. He was sure she had personal problems but was not the type who would readily put them around; he still felt sure that she could help with his problem over Janine.

She sipped her coffee, and said with a smile, 'Honestly, Mark, I feel a bit of a fraud, you bringing me out like this tonight; I really don't know if I can be of any use to you. My own life has been terribly dull. I can put it into three words. School, training and hospital.'

He gave another laugh which seemed to convey all the wisdom, compassion and broad-mindedness of his character, and yet she knew there was a stubbornness and iron will beneath that charming façade. Even so, now a certain weakness was emerging about him regarding Janine. It was as if, much as he admired women, there were some from whom he would rather run a mile! Maybe she was quite wrong, but the image certainly made her give a silent little chuckle.

'You know, I honestly believe you have me on a piece of string with those three words, Katy! Your life has probably been one of high adventure!'

'If only,' she laughed lightly. 'It seems to me that yours has been already, from what you've told me tonight—a ship's doctor following in your father's footsteps, a five-year stint back home at Manchester General, California, then running the English hospital in Brunei for nearly seven years.'

'Not a bit of it. At times it was all boring to distraction; that's how I came to fall so heavily for Janine's charms, I suppose.' He leaned forward suddenly, cradling the coffee cup between long, slender fingers, then placed it back on the saucer with a small sigh. 'Well, I must say that your own potted biography is minuscule if it's true,' he teased. 'What about this boyfriend of yours?'

'What about him?' she said pertly. Her heart lurched. She knew he was only being friendly about the fictional boyfriend, but even now, two years on, a direct question always seemed to drive her into a corner. Her stomach fluttered and the old fear began to take over—fear of someone having read about her in a newspaper all that time ago, fear of people remembering her 'married' name and the details lapped up in court by London journalists hard up for a story, fear of those journalists maybe chasing a 'before and after' saga when well-known names were thin on the ground. She drew a deep breath, waiting for his response. . .

But he was shaking his head. 'Sorry, Katy, I was out of order there, I had no right to ask the question. It has nothing to do with me, and you've every right to tell me so,' he said quietly, the lost look in her eyes still getting to him. 'But even so I want to thank you for the help you gave me when Janine turned up the other day, and with the odd phone calls too for that matter.'

'No, please, Mark, it was nothing.'

A small frown had settled between his eyes. 'Anyhow, I must put you in the picture about this whole business. You see, it all goes back to Brunei really. Once I had settled down after the first few months, there were invitations for the usual social round, and Janine—who lived there with her barrister father, her mother having died years before while she'd been away at school—was very friendly.

'For a while a crowd of us went around together—swimming, tennis, riding, all the usual things whenever I could manage it. I thought little of her, until one morning I had a call from her saying the crowd had organised a picnic for the following day on the beach, and would I care to join them. . .'

He sat back in his chair. 'I gladly agreed to go on this trip with the others,' he said, his eyes taking on a far-away look, as if he had transported himself back to that exotic land. 'Next morning, the arrangement was that we all met at my place—I had a house in the hospital grounds, plenty of room for cars et cetera—when to my surprise I saw only Janine arrive. Airily she explained that the trip had been cancelled owing to several friends being due to take part in a polo match that day, and it having quite slipped their mind. Janine, it seemed, had everything we needed for the picnic, and so, after I'd accepted her explanation, off we went.

'The entire trip had been a figment of her imagination, and, brazen as she was, she told me she preferred just the two of us anyway, which I had no reason to mind! The beach was called Pantai-Tungko—Prince's Beach—a magnificent sweep of golden sand stippled with sandy coves and rocks, an idyllic place in which to swim and relax. I have to say, Katy, that on that day I was quite mesmerised by Janine's charms. From then on the relationship developed into a very turbulent affair.'

He gave a small, ironic smile. 'Yes, I know I lost my head. . . I was crazy. . .'

'Did it go on for long?'

'Too long, I'm afraid. Jealousy reared its ugly head—on Janine's part in the form of a very domineering streak, not that she didn't conceal it very effectively for some time. Then I began to hear gossip about her past. At first I refused to listen, until I realised that despite her possessiveness she was two-timing me. One night we had a fearsome row, and she flung herself at my feet in hysterical tears, saying it was only because she loved me so much and was trying to make me jealous.'

He gave a huge sigh. 'I know it sounds harsh, Katy, but it hadn't taken long for me to realise the net was tightening and I had to get away, to get back home to work. Janine guessed, and from then on made my life hell; I just couldn't reason with her. . .'

Katy looked at Mark's taut expression, not disbelieving him but trying to imagine this girl chasing after a man so attractive and his obviously resenting her attentions. . . For a brief moment, something in her own heart made her feel sorry for the girl, and she remembered her own rejection. But that's where the comparison ended. In her case, she now realised, it had been infatuation, not love. 'Did you try to explain that the affair had blown itself out, Mark?'

He shook his head in despair. 'Katy, I did everything on God's earth I could think of to make her see sense. Even my superiors had commiserated with me, apparently knowing Janine far better than I, and to my eternal thanks they managed to arrange that I got away sooner than was usual in such a job.

'Fortunately my replacement had no family ties and he was therefore able to take my place earlier than I'd hoped. Ultimately came the farewell parties. Janine was there, as sweetly charming as she can be, especially when she's been drinking. Nevertheless, I felt I was awaiting a volcanic eruption. The final party and dance that evening had been too uneventful as far as Janine was concerned. She was too submissive, far too delightful and I was convinced that she was a pretty good actress.

'When I left the party because I had an early flight the following morning, Janine said her goodbyes like everyone else; I was so surprised that I was almost tempted to invite her back to my place for a final word, but common sense prevailed and I passed up the idea.'

Katy noticed a small blue vein working at Mark's temple, his jaw clenched as he went on. 'It was well after midnight when she turned up at my place in her car, as drunk as I'd ever seen her as she fell through the open front door of my house. It was an exceptionally hot night; the cicadas were making the devil of a din. . . I'll never forget that night as long as I live. . .' He ran a distraught hand across his hair, gazing into the middle distance.

'Mark,' she said gently, 'would you rather not carry on with this?'

'No, Katy, I must finish. In fact there is not a lot more to say. I'd long since fallen out of love with her.

She had simply been flirting with anyone who was interested and—well, I don't intend going into all the sordid details.

'Hence my shock when she telephoned. On my first night at Rosewall I had the call from Brunei.' He smiled. 'That's when you and I headed for the same telephone. . . It was one of my friends from the hospital, warning me of Janine's intentions. The shock being that I had not realised she would show up here quite so soon.' He spread out his hands, looking at Katy, anxiety mixed with regret on his face. 'And you know the rest,' he said simply.

'It's certainly a sad story,' Katy murmured. 'Was she English born?'

'Oh, yes. Her parents moved to Brunei when she was about five years old and quite spoilt her, I believe. She never had a job, although she did qualify as a physiotherapist; I suppose it was that which gave us something in common in the first place. Apparently her father seemed to crack up when her mother died. Janine was in her teens and Basil Harper then took to drink, I'm afraid. Great pity—he was damned good at his job. Retired now, though.'

'So you had no idea that Janine was going to follow you over here to Maldon—seriously, I mean?'

'None whatsoever. She threatened as much during the weeks leading up to my leaving, but I couldn't take her seriously.' His face held one of his withdrawn expressions, as if he wanted to say a great deal yet was hesitating at the wisdom of it. He asked quickly, 'Katy, just out of interest, what is your opinion on jealousy between two people?'

Taken aback, she didn't answer immediately but was transfixed by the intensity of his words. He obviously wasn't expecting a flippant reply, the sort she herself had hidden behind more recently. And yet a small voice inside warned her not to be naïve either, to remember how she had put her trust in Steve when they had talked things over together, and she had believed him, followed by his shattering let-down. . .

Mark was watching her as she raised an eyebrow, shrugging a slim shoulder nonchalantly, saying, 'I don't really have a set opinion on such a loaded topic, Mark—between friends, you understand. All I know is that some folk think love is for the taking just when they want it, but jealousy is something again—a pointless emotion that feeds upon itself and grows into a monster.'

She smiled brightly, disregarding the still, stern set look on his face. 'So,' she continued, 'why put oneself into a no-win situation? Metaphorically I'm talking of a person who is beset with jealousy over the other, whereas so often the subject of that emotion may be quite unable to comprehend such thinking. Even worse, to be totally unaware of it. . .'

Suddenly she felt as if she was walking a tightrope, comparing something of her own traumatic experience with that of Janine and Mark, about whom she knew very little and possibly only the tip of the iceberg. She smiled into Mark's eyes, widening her own so that the brilliant blue entranced him briefly, but at the same time giving the impression that that was her considered opinion and no more.

Katy couldn't be sure if it was exasperation that sent a horizontal crease across his brow as he pondered her words before saying tersely, 'Forgive me, Katy, but I would suggest, with respect, that you have never been mixed up in that particular hell.'

The words were almost wrenched from him. It was an admonishment that she had never known the sort of possessive love that created real jealousy. At least, she thought, she now had some inkling of Janine's make-up.

'Fortunately, Mark, you are right,' she agreed. 'Has it ever happened to you or are you a more equable person when it comes to true love?' she asked lightly.

He grinned suddenly. 'Goodness knows, Katy! But I do know that you are quite a diplomat in your way!' Mark ordered fresh coffee for them both from a passing waiter. 'Time for a little break, I think; we've been getting rather serious.'

She was glad of the coffee, now feeling more at ease with him as she said, 'About Janine, Mark—I was with a friend in town the other evening actually; I think I saw you both leaving the hotel there, the one in the main street. Were you able to smooth a few things out with regard to her unexpected appearance?'

He shook his head vigorously. ''Fraid not; I only delayed things by a lot of talk which she'll not be put off by for too long. She will not see reason, and there's no logic in her thinking. I tried to convince her that our relationship ended long ago, that we could still remain friends in whichever part of the world we find ourselves. She appeared to go along with that, but then suggested that perhaps we might meet now and again. To avoid a scene in the hotel I agreed to that. It seemed a simple enough request, but as you know she turned up at the hospital again this morning still demanding to see me. That, of course, is the problem; Janine makes up the rules as she goes along. I never know what she will do next, and the big trouble I foresee is that she may place my job in jeopardy, especially as she has come over here and is not going to get what she wants. She will stop at nothing, particularly knowing how much my job means to me.'

He drank his coffee down in one long draught. 'This is the reason I wanted to talk to you, Katy. We haven't known each other very long, I know, but you always seem such a level-headed person to me, and, well, just talking things through with you is greatly appreciated, I assure you. It isn't that I cannot handle Janine in one sense, but I simply wanted an impartial opinion on something that is so very personal and yet so important to my carrying on here at Rosewall. . .'

'I know what you mean, of course, Mark. I wonder. . .'

'Yes?' he asked keenly.

'Well, I just wondered whether if you brought her along to the Prof's party tomorrow evening it would convince her that you were not trying to shut her out, as she probably thinks, or that you're ignoring her. It might at least make it appear that you've kept to your side of the bargain.'

Mark made a wry face. 'Well, I told her this morning I didn't know when I was going to see her again, but I can always change my mind. In fact,' he said slowly, 'it might be quite a possibility.'

Janine did not enter their conversation any further, and Mark was by now full of apologies for the way he had taken up Katy's time. 'I had no idea it was so late, Katy, I am really sorry.'

As they left the Old Barge to get into the car, Katy was still trying to convince him otherwise. 'Mark, for heaven's sake, if we can't help each other it's a miserable world, and one thing I want to say is that nothing of what we have said will go any further.'

They seemed to reach the hospital again in no time. Mark drew to a stop outside the nurses' home, cutting the car engine and looking at her with gratitude. 'I can't thank you enough for your help in this business, Katy. Even if it does work out as we'd hoped, I still think you're great the way you've been so generous with your time when I know your own family needs you.'

Katy smiled. 'Don't worry. Next weekend I hope to be going home to Clacton so we'll have plenty of time to talk then.'

Mark stepped out of the vehicle, opening her door, taking her hand as she got out, being slow to release it, and saying warmly, 'Goodnight, Katy.

See you tomorrow at the party, apart from work, of course.'

Next morning on Fortune things seemed relatively quiet, and, best of all, there was a note in Katy's office from the decorators, saying they would be moving out that day, after putting everything back in its place under staff supervision. 'Thank heaven for that!' Katy said happily to Tessa as they met in the cloakroom. 'It shouldn't take us too long to get everything straight again!'

Tessa slipped out of her jacket and brushed her hair. 'I have quite good news too! Roger's wife is going to stay with a relative this weekend, and he'll be able to come to the Professor's party.'

'Oh, great, Tess.'

Still talking, the two girls left the cloakroom, only to be concerned by a commotion breaking out in the newly decorated ward; a lot of shouting was going on, and a small group of people, including the decorators, were sympathising with someone who was lying sprawled on the floor. 'Oh, dear,' Katy murmured, 'why did this have to happen? Let's go and see. . .'

Tess gasped as they neared the group; a man was lying on the floor, his leg twisted unnaturally, his face turned away from them. Tess said quickly, 'Good heavens, it's poor old Ron Green! What's he doing up here anyway?'

Katy quickly went to the young man's aid. 'Hi, Ron, what the devil have you been doing?'

'Katy,' he moaned, 'I have a hell of a pain in my ankle; I think I've broken it; look how swollen it is. . .'

'Tess, quickly collect a wheelchair, will you, and get Ron down to A and E? I'll ring Joanna and tell her you're coming.'

'How the heck did you do this, Ron? Were there only the decorators here?' she asked, while Melanie, who had just appeared, helped him up to a sitting position.

'I'll tell you later, Katy. Besides,' he said, grimacing with pain, 'I don't want Joanna to know all the ins and outs when we get down to A and E, do I?'

'She's got to know how it happened; you must know that, of all people. . .'

His face was contorted with pain as Tessa arrived, and Katy, with Melanie's help, transferred him to the chair. On the phone Joanna said, 'Bring him down straight away; Mr Hammond's down here, as it happens.'

'OK,' Katy said, hurrying to press the button for the lift. 'Don't worry, Ron; it may just be a bad sprain.'

The spokesman for the decorators was looking very worried, and hurried up to Katy as soon as she was free. 'I'm right sorry about this, Sister; we didn't know 'e was coming in 'ere. We'd just started setting things straight, like, and, unknown to us, a tin of paint which we thought was empty had been overlooked when we tidied up last night. We can only guess it had been on its side all night, covered up, and no one noticed the paint trickling out of it. This morning, one of my men was taking the dust covers off, didn't notice this puddle o' paint on the floor, and then this guy came in and the next thing I knew he'd gone down on his backside and twisted in a nasty fall. . .'

'Oh, dear, I see. Well, thanks very much for telling me. I'll have to let Miss Munro, the SNO, know, and she'll no doubt want you to fill in a form of some sort before you leave.'

The kindly man looked worried. 'OK, right. Well, I can't see how it was our fault, Sister; we didn't ask this guy to come in.'

Later, Katy made a mental note to go down to visit Ron Green. From then on the rest of the staff gave a hand with getting the newly furbished ward straight, along with all the beds with their new curtains and counterpanes in a cheerful turquoise flowery material. Katy preferred the gold on Fortune, but then Miss Munro's choice was her own and she obviously liked floral. While Katy was putting finishing touches to the linen, her office telephone rang.

'Sister Woods. . .'

'Oh, hi, Katy—Joanna! Our patient has just gone into Theatre for plastering; he's got a second-degree sprain there. We did a radiograph. Torn ligaments, I'm afraid, but he hasn't displaced the joint. There were also a few chips of bone. Jolly painful. Mr Hammond has given the ankle a local anaesthetic, which will afford some temporary relief. That's the report, Katy. I'm afraid you'll no doubt hear it from Mr Hammond. Ron's an idiot; what was he doing up in your place anyway, Katy?'

Katy suddenly had a recollection of Ron Green's woeful face.

'I couldn't really tell you, Joanna, but I reckon after a couple of days or so he'll be only too delighted to put you in the picture.'

'I've just remembered how he was plaguing me to go to the Professor's party tonight. Poor guy, that's gone for a burton, hasn't it? Oh, well, there's a new houseman who's asked me. He'll do, I suppose, if I can get the time off!'

By the time Katy had filled in the forms regarding the accident, and Miss Munro had been upstairs herself and reviewed the situation, the day was almost half over. Mark Hammond arrived late after being in the theatre, and looked decidedly withdrawn when Katy took him in to see Janet Stacey. 'How is she?' Mark asked as they went into Fortune Ward.

'Downhearted, from what I can gather from Night Sister.'

'You mean with regard to her going home for the weekend?'

'Yes.'

'But she doesn't know what I'm going to say yet, does she?'

'She says she has a premonition!'

Mark Hammond didn't smile as he might have done normally, and Katy could only conclude that he was worrying about the Professor's party that evening. After asking Mrs Stacey one or two pertinent questions and being given the answers, Mark Hammond heaved a short sigh. 'You know, Mrs Stacey,' he said, putting his pen away, 'I'm going to have to say no to going home on this particular occasion. You have only been in here with us for less than a fortnight. Your blood pressure is still too high, and excitement of any kind could be extremely dangerous. . .'

'How dangerous, Doctor?' Janet Stacey said tearfully.

'Your baby could die, to put it bluntly, and I know that you're sensible enough to realise that nothing is worth taking that sort of risk for.'

She blew her nose, shaking her head. 'No, I understand, of course. My Pete will agree. Tonight I hope to hear the result of his talk with Tina, so perhaps it's just as well.'

Back in the office, Mark Hammond slumped down in a chair at the desk. 'Poor Mrs Stacey,' he said to Katy. 'I hope she begins to see how sensible she's being.' He gave a wry grin. 'I wish I could solve my troubles as easily!'

Katy grinned. 'You may be in for a pleasant surprise yet.' She took the prescriptions he'd signed for her. 'Charge Nurse Ron Green's having an unlucky day too, isn't he?'

'Yes, damned painful ankle he'll have for a while.' He looked at her, sombrely, his long jaw impressive, the shapely lips slightly upturned. 'He's going to be in the men's ward downstairs for a couple of days; that plaster may be a problem at first, but we'll just have to wait and see.' He stood up suddenly. 'By the way, you can imagine the rather over-ecstatic response I had from Janine when I rang her at the hotel last night. She has accepted the invitation, of course, and I'm picking her up at seven. Are you OK for a lift?'

'Thanks so much, yes, several of us are piling into Roger's Range Rover.'

'Good. I'll see you later on this evening, then.' He left the office, the withdrawn expression soon settling back on his face. Katy sighed too, wondering what this Janine would be like face to face, and also how some of the other guests might view Mr Mark Hammond's 'friend', for at this point Katy knew of only one or two people who had experienced any contact with her.

In her room that evening, Katy dressed thoughtfully; these parties were quite pleasant affairs although they did not require over-dressing. She glanced at the new slim-fitting black dress she had bought in town, fairly short with brief sleeves, and black sequins scattered on the oval neckline. It was just about right, she hoped. Medium-heeled sandals completed the outfit, and with her fair hair on her shoulders she felt fairly confident that her purchases had been justified. As she ran downstairs she made a firm resolution that she would not prejudge Janine but treat her as if she knew nothing whatsoever about her.

CHAPTER FIVE

THE Professor's house was a large, rambling family home, square and solid, its white walls covered with ivy and the front door framed with climbing white and mauve clematis—the sort of dwelling that simply lent itself to any social occasion.

As the party from Rosewall drove in, the gravel drive was already practically full of vehicles, and the gardener directed Roger, Tess and Katy into the small paddock nearby; they were closely followed by Mark and Janine. Janine, tall, elegant and extremely attractive, was obviously doing her best to take in her surroundings with a lively interest.

As they all stepped from the car, Katy smiled at her warmly, at the same time thinking what an ideal couple she and Mark made. 'Hello, Janine.' Katy smiled again. 'I'm sure you'll soon sort us all out. Let's go into the cloakroom, shall we, and let the men fend for themselves? You lead the way, Tess!'

Upstairs one of Rupert Mason's four unmarried daughters, who were all in various branches of the medical profession, was helping everyone with the usual array of coats and wraps. Janine, who had flung off a flamboyant Malaysian wrap from her slim-fitting peacock-blue dress, deftly touched the dark, shining abundance of her hair dressed in a smooth chignon style and needing little attention, saying to Katy as she turned from the mirror, 'You know I'm so glad to meet you and your colleagues, Katy; Mark has talked such a lot about you, I feel that we're friends already.'

'That's great, Janine! I do hope you are going to enjoy your holiday here.'

Janine's almond-shaped eyes, high cheekbones and full sensuous mouth combined into a dazzling smile that encompassed Katy with earnest friendliness. 'Oh, Katy, you are so kind to me! I know it's silly, but when Mark told me he was bringing me here to meet you I felt quite nervous; now I see there's just no reason to be that way at all!'

'Heavens, no, Janine,' Tess said, collecting up her handbag and heading for the door, at the same time smiling her thanks to the Professor's daughter. 'You certainly didn't have to feel that way, everyone's so very nice here.'

'Yes, I see that now,' Janine said as they went downstairs together to the large drawing room where the party was being held and Rupert and Kathleen Mason, with various members of their large family, were congregated.

Mark met Janine, and she linked her arm with his, giving him quite a radiant smile which surprised Katy, but she soon forgot the incident when Roger and another anaesthetist friend of his, Peter Oliver, moved to join the large group now forming in readiness for the Professor's presentation.

Miss Munro, plus several worthies of the hospital committee, began the speeches, which were both witty and succinct, to which the Professor replied with equal humour and brevity, particularly on being given a complete set of expensive-looking fishing rods and even a canvas igloo tent for two to go with them.

For one silent moment he was quite overcome, and had to pause before being able to express his surprise and gratitude. Amidst applause, he said with a smile, placing an arm around his wife's shoulders, 'My Kathleen has been a wonderful wife—so much so that our children are too comfortable at home to get married; that's how good she's been. . .' He paused again amidst laughter. 'But now I can assure you that we certainly will be getting away on our own with this wonderful gift from you all, and. . .'

Further speeches were added, followed by music and an excellent buffet; drinks flowed, and the evening was deemed a great success. Katy realised suddenly that Mark was at her side, while Janine was engaged in an animated conversation with the Professor and his wife.

At least Mark was looking slightly less agitated, saying beneath his breath, with a relieved smile, 'Well, so far, so good!'

'Everything's fine, Mark. Janine seems to be quite at home with us,' Katy answered.

Mark shook his head. 'Take it from me, Katy, she's got something up her sleeve.'

Katy felt a small spark of irritation. 'I don't imagine so, somehow, Mark.' He didn't answer, and again she felt a small niggle of doubt about this girl of whom Mark had told her so much, but it seemed incomprehensible now, on seeing her laughing and talking in such an easy manner with Rupert and Kathleen, and previously with the rest of the party too, for that matter. Surely it was possible that Mark himself might be just somewhat over-wrought, and the girl had no idea of chasing after him from Brunei in that sense? It might just be possible that she had come to Britain for a totally different reason, and at the same time had decided to see him for old times' sake.

Ultimately the evening drew to a pleasant close and people began to leave gradually; Mark said he would be running Janine back to her hotel, and all goodbyes were said as Tess, Roger and Katy accompanied Janine and Mark back to their car in the paddock.

Janine was talking animatedly to Mark, when Katy overheard her telling him about Kathleen's invitation to dinner to them both. Then in a very fractious voice she said, 'Oh, do let's tell them, darling. . .'

Mark's clipped voice rose on the cool night air as

the two got into the car. 'Oh, for heaven's sake, don't be so ridiculous, Janine!' His car door slammed, but the windows were down. 'Why is it you must always dramatise everything? Leave things as they are and forget it!'

'Forget it? You say forget it?' Janine's voice was rising to a high-pitched crescendo, but their car moved almost parallel with the others and at the same time she lowered her voice to a charming pitch, calling, 'Bye now! Bye! Great seeing you. . . Tremendous evening!'

'Bye, Janine. . . Mark. . .'

'What do you think all that was about?' Roger said as they set off in the Range Rover.

Tess was looking at Katy with raised eyebrows. 'No idea at all, Rog. Some little hiccup between the two of them, no doubt.'

'A lover's tiff, perhaps,' Tessa sang out airily. It took only a short time to reach the nurses' home. 'Katy. . .um. . .I have told Rog about our talk. . .'

Katy turned, and smiled at them both. 'Bless you, my children; my lips are sealed!'

Roger grinned happily. 'Some day one of us is going to be rewarded in heaven, and it has to be you, Katy!'

'Never,' she laughed, leaving the car. 'Thanks so much for the lift, both of you. Super evening. Bye now!'

Once in her room, Katy closed the door behind her thoughtfully, pondering upon the evening and the way it had gone, followed by what she had heard between Mark and Janine. It was obviously something that was a bone of contention between them and which they had managed to keep at bay during the party, and it seemed to have a bearing on their being invited to the Professor's to dinner at some future date.

In her minuscule bedroom off the sitting room, Katy threw down her things on the bed with a sigh. She was still unsure about the knowledge she had regarding the relationship between Mark and Janine; in fact it was a difficult situation to find herself in. Saying what she really thought, as Mark had suggested, was tricky, and already she was beginning to wish that she had not been involved, despite the fact that her undiminishing attraction for him seemed to weaken all her resolve. . .

She shrugged, deciding to make herself a cup of coffee. She was certainly not ready for bed; sleep was furthest from her mind. For no reason at all she had a fleeting recollection of Peter Oliver that evening. As a friend of Roger's, he seemed quite a nice gregarious type, and had told her that he worked mostly at Colchester General. She knew he had driven over by car, and had had to leave early to pick up a member of staff and drive back to Colchester that evening. Pity. She felt so unsettled at present, she could almost have invited him back for a drink.

Yet the crazy thought was chased away as soon as it was formed in her mind. She had enough complications for the time being as it was. . .

The phone suddenly split the silence. She glanced at her wrist-watch—almost midnight.

Don't let it be trouble, she prayed, thinking of Ross and the possibility that Fleur might have suffered a relapse of some kind. She lifted the receiver. 'Hello, yes. . . ?'

'Katy, it's Mark.' The deep voice was unmistakable. 'Forgive me; I was wondering if you were feeling sleepless like me?'

A lovely warmth had wrapped itself about Katy. 'Exactly the same as you, Mark.' She smiled. 'What do you think we can do about it?' Her voice sounded husky, seductive almost, although she was hardly aware of it.

'You could tell me that you feel like going along the beach tonight,' he said quietly.

'Is there a moon?' she murmured.

'I can't honestly remember; I don't think so. In that

case, no beach. I also have a reasonable flat but not at all to my liking, so I shall delay that particular invitation to you.'

'Yes, that might cause some gossip, which I'm sure would be thoroughly unjustified!'

'Oh, but definitely! Never let it be said that the staff of Fortune would indulge in anything so. . .so mundane!'

His low chuckle suddenly sounded easy, as if he had had quite a battle with himself as to whether or not he should ring her at so late an hour and had now relaxed. 'We are no ordinary people, you know, Sister Woods!' he teased. 'And, for that very reason, I say to you that tonight I am feeling decidedly odd and unable to sleep, and I see nothing wrong in a friend of yours calling upon you.'

'Now that, Mr Hammond, is an extremely sensible idea; I wonder why we didn't get round to it in the first place? If you can be here in five minutes, I'll have the coffee on!'

Katy flew around the kitchen for the next three minutes, leaving two to spare to plump the cushions and put out three of the brightest lights, leaving only the side-lamps on by the settee before going downstairs and opening the outer door of the building. It was perfect timing. Mark stood there in his dinner suit, so handsome that she was riveted to the spot, until she remembered that beneath all their banter was probably some quite serious reason for his visit.

'Do come upstairs, Mark.' They went up and she pushed open her door, the room in a mellow flood of gold, the electric-fire logs glowing on the cream curtains drawn across the night. And there was a welcoming fragrance of coffee as Katy brought in the tray.

Mark pulled the small table forward as they sat down. He gave a wry grin, saying soberly, 'This is so good of you, Katy.'

She handed him a cup, her fair hair gleaming in the firelight. 'Mark—and this is absolutely true—I could not sleep either, and as the phone rang I was just about to make some coffee. Really!'

He smiled into her eyes, glancing at the black dress in which she had tantalised him all evening. 'I don't think in my whole life that I have ever been so blatantly selfish, Katy. I hardly said a word to you this evening; there just wasn't a chance. I knew when we left the Masons', there would be little sleep for me tonight. Please don't think, though, that I am inflicting my insomnia upon you. Heaven forbid! It's just that Janine has done what she set out to do. . .' He drank his coffee, all laughter and lightness gone from his voice. 'It's the subtlety of it which warns me that she has changed very little.'

Katy tucked her long, slender legs up beneath her on the settee. 'But Mark, she was charming enough, or so it seemed to me. Everyone was very impressed, and I'm sure they think there's something between you and Janine.' Quite suddenly—maybe it was the still of the night that made her feel bold and able to say what she truly felt—she added, 'Isn't it likely that, given the different environment in which we live here, Mark, you could both. . .start again in a sense? I mean, after all, there was a great deal that attracted you to each other in the beginning. . .'

She shook her head lightly. 'Oh, dear, I shouldn't be saying such things, but I'd hate to hear of all these personal wrangles and then learn later that you were really right for each other after all. It would be so wrong for me to. . .sort of. . .be a party to it. . . Surely you understand how I feel, Mark?'

He sat, hands clasped loosely between his knees, the fine head turned in strong profile, pensive, taking in her words, yet unable to tell her the half of it. . . He gave a huge sigh, holding her hand in his, gently running his fingers along hers, admiring the velvet skin, the beautiful filbert-shaped nails. 'Katy, my having put my confidence in you—has it become too much of a burden? Because if it is going to worry you greatly I will stop immediately. In the first instance I was so impressed by your understanding when Janine arrived back here at the outset, I thought, perhaps—well, that I was the weaker of the two and from the feminine point of view you could see far more than I. . .'

She relaxed back upon the cushions, sorting out her thoughts, trying not to be conscious of the length of his thigh against her own as they sat together. His dark eyes turned to hers, almost indigo in the shadowy lamplight, how she wished she knew what he was thinking. Was he attracted to her physically? Did she amuse him? Did he like her appearance? There had been hints. . .

She pulled herself together. Wasn't she supposed to be helping the poor guy out of a difficult situation that could cost him his job, just because some silly, empty-headed woman had played around until she tired of him, then when it suited her had begun the chase all over again. . . ?

'Mark,' she said suddenly, 'I happened to overhear something Janine said when you were leaving the Masons' in the car. Is it that which is worrying you tonight?'

'To be honest, Katy, yes, it is.'

'Of course I couldn't put it in context—I overheard only the briefest of words—but I have to confess I was surprised that she sounded so waspish when during the whole of the evening she had been so totally different.'

'I don't want to say "I told you so", Katy, and, as you so rightly remind me, how are you to know that I may not enlist your help for the two of us, and that we won't then quite suddenly change our minds?' He gave a hollow laugh. 'Quite a scenario, but not one that is going to happen. She is, of course, quite delighted with the invitation to the Masons' in a week or so, and therefore is wanting to give a hint that we are—as one might say—having a relationship. The whole thing is ludicrous, and what's worrying me now is the fact that she may become too sure of herself here now—and there's no telling when she'll take her leave.'

Katy could see that his spirits had flagged badly since their joking on the phone, and it was easy to realise why when he had obviously had enough of this woman's wiles. 'Mark,' she said, 'I think that the only thing you can do is to make this coming dinner invitation the culmination, as it were, of her trip, and then insist that you can no longer have her on hand in this way because your work comes first. Also, suggest that while she's in this country she does some touring around before returning home to Brunei.'

Mark was already shaking his head with a stubborn, drawn expression on his face. 'No, Katy, that is all far too civilised for her. It won't work. There is only one way, as I see it, and that is to be utterly ruthless and tell her in no uncertain terms that I have no further interest in her and that she must accept my word in that respect.'

'If you think that's best.'

'Do you know who else will be at the Masons' dinner?' Mark asked.

'Not yet, but usually a sprinkling of staff attend, as well as other guests.'

Mark sat for a second staring at the soft mushroom carpet, his mind obviously a million miles away, judging by his expression; then he said brusquely, 'Well, I can tell you, Katy, this will positively be the last and final occasion I shall accompany her anywhere.' The hard expression left his features as he turned to smile at her, as if the subject was now closed.

Then the strong face broke into a soft smiles, and he said brightly, 'Let's talk about something else! This boyfriend you've mentioned, Katy—you rarely speak of him. Forgive me, but he does not seem to play a great part in your life.' He gave a small upswing of his lips. 'And, believe it or not, now I am beginning to worry about you!'

Katy felt herself blush. She had wondered when this question would arise, and, having got to know the man who had started to haunt her dreams, it didn't seem such a dire confession to make any more. She had never forgotten how, on the first night he'd arrived at the hospital, she had experienced an incredible feeling of wanting to talk many things over with him, as if it was the most natural thing in the world.

She had never fully been able to understand it. After all, at that particular time he was a total stranger, not least her superior in the work hierarchy; in that respect he still was, and she knew that her work satisfied him, and they seemed to think in unison when there were problems to be handled.

In the same way, she now knew he trusted her with his private worries and concerns, having appealed to her as he had for her help. Now, maybe, he wanted to redress the balance. Was that so very terrible? She felt sure he asked without any idea of prying but simply because they had become real friends.

She realised that his dark, long-lashed eyes were upon her, waiting for a reply. . . 'Mark,' she said, glancing from his penetrating gaze, 'I'm afraid that for various reasons the boyfriend was quite fictional; suffice it to say that there are times when it is useful for a girl to resort to this. Also. . .also. . .'

She took a deep breath, poised as she was on the brink of the whole story about Steve, but hovered and stopped herself. 'I would tell you why this was necessary at the outset, but it is rather late now, and maybe it would be better some other time. It is simply that, having fought my way through a very bad time myself in the. . .in the love stakes, it was necessary to have some kind of shield against ever getting into a similar situation again.'

He turned towards her, his long, slender fingers tracing the beautiful outline of her face, then took her hand in his, and the way her heart leapt at the contact seemed to deny her statement about ever falling in love again, but how could he know what she felt merely at the touch of his hand. . . ?

'Katy, I cannot say that I'm surprised. Ever since I first saw you I have wondered about the sadness in those fantastic eyes of yours. I agree it is far too late this evening to go into anything of that kind, but, whenever you feel the need to talk, you know that I'm here. You have been so generous about Janine and me, and I suspect, had I known exactly what your problem was, I would have hesitated to trouble you with mine.'

Katy stood up quickly, feeling his closeness and the intimacy of the room to be almost too much. 'How about a whisky before you go, Mark? It might help you to sleep tonight.'

He rose to his feet, the slim elegance of him making her breath flutter in her throat as he said with a smile, 'Only if you'll join me.'

'Why not?' She poured the drinks, her hand shaking slightly as he strolled over to where she stood at the small bottle cabinet. His proximity, a faint suggestion of aftershave, the points of a crisp white handkerchief just visible at his breast pocket all combined to make her oblivious to what she was doing.

They each sipped their drink, toasting each other with their eyes; it was a moment in time held suspended between them, until he took both glasses and set them aside, cupped her oval face with its frame of long fair hair between his hands, his eyes holding hers as he murmured, 'I could tell that you have been Miss Independent for a while, and in view of what you have told me tonight, Katy, I think you should relent a little now and enjoy all the admiration you can get. . . Like this. . .'

Slowly, hands on her shoulders, he drew her to him, his gaze going over her, lingering on the charm of her lips, her neck and the honey-coloured rise of her breasts. The shadowy cleft between them, the gentle thud of her quivering heartbeats were not concealed from Mark's eye as tenderly his arms went around her. Her body was pressed against his when, light as gossamer, his lips brushed hers, and again.

She no longer questioned what she was doing but with a small inner groan stretched her soft contours along Mark's sinewy litheness as their lips met now in one long and passionate kiss. . . His tongue made contact with hers. . . She broke away quickly, gasping, saying laughingly, 'I'm afraid I'm not a very good hostess, Mark. Can I. . .can I get you a top-up?' she asked, looking at his glass.

He smiled at the glorious flush of colour in her cheeks, the brilliance of her eyes, and slightly ruffled hair. 'At this moment, Katy, I would say there could not be another hostess anywhere in the world as lovely as you! Thank you for the offer anyway, but I'll stay no longer.' He brushed her cheek with the back of his hand. 'Thank you for this last hour with you. I can't tell you how much it means to me. In fact you have made me feel a whole lot better.'

They moved towards the door. 'I'll let myself out,' he said in a low voice. 'See you tomorrow at work, and remember we have a date to keep, if you want to, that is.' Gently he placed his hands upon her slim shoulders, saying, 'Certainly I should like it very much.' He drew back from her with difficulty. . .

Katy's mind too was in a turmoil; she could hardly trust herself to speak, and tried to keep her reply very low-key. 'Well, we are good friends, Mark, after all. . .'

With a gentle smile, he whispered, 'Goodnight, Katy,' and, dropping a kiss on her cheek, went through the door.

Back in her room, Katy hardly knew what to think first, but, in the event, she undressed in something of a daze, then fell into bed in a dreamless sleep.

Next day was Sunday; it was warm and sunny and quite an effort not to think of the beach. Katy collected the few letters for Fortune, and before going upstairs to the third floor made her way to the men's ward to see Ron Green on the first. Having gained permission to do so, Katy went along to the two-bedded units and found him sitting up scouring the morning newspapers, having already finished his breakfast.

'Hi, Ron! How's our celebrated patient this morning?'

'Coo! Celebrated! What we do to go after birds, eh, Katy? 'Cos you know that's what I was doing, don't you, up there in your ward when it all happened?'

'Well. . .'

'Oh, come on; old Joanna has told you all about me, I bet!'

'Maybe!' Katy said quickly, glancing at her fob-watch. 'How's the ankle, anyway? That's what I came up to see about.'

Ron Green wrinkled his nose, and the thought went through Katy's mind that he was still too good-looking for his own vanity, despite the grimace and shaking his head. 'Do you know, Katy, I'd never have believed that this injury could have been so ruddy painful?' he said miserably, the mask of bravado falling briefly. 'With a bit of luck, though, I might be going home in about a week, after I've knocked about here in a wheelchair for a few days.'

'Good heavens!' Katy exploded playfully. 'I hope everyone's been warned, especially Joanna!'

'Rotten luck I missed the Prof's do, though, wasn't it? Especially when I'd asked Joanna to go with me. How did it go last evening?'

'Very good. . .' She told him all the details he might be interested in, and was about to leave when he said quickly, 'Be a pal, Katy—give Joanna this note for me, would you?'

'Can't you put it in the postbox?'

'What, and waste a stamp? Not so likely!' He grinned suddenly. 'Do you know, I always thought you were a bit stuck-up, Katy, but I've changed my mind. I reckon you're a bit of all right. . .' he called as she took his note and waved him goodbye. She knew she would be seeing Joanna at lunch so decided to give it to her then. Joanna would probably blush to the tips of her ears, considering how hard she tried to dismiss Ron Green when Katy teased her about him.

When Katy got to her office the telephone was ringing. She picked up the instrument, absently touching the burnished-bronze chrysanthemums in a jug on her desk. 'Sister Woods speaking.'

'Hello, Katy. Miss Munro. Did you enjoy yourself at the Professor's party last night?'

'Very much, thanks, Miss Munro; I thought it all went off very well. And you?'

'Oh, extremely pleasant. As a matter of fact, that's rather what I'm ringing about. I've had a call from Kathleen Mason this morning; she tells me she has invited Mark Hammond and his friend Janine to dinner in a week's time, and wanted to know if you knew anything about her relationship with Mr Hammond. I think Kathleen feels a little uneasy with not knowing too much about her, particularly as she seemed, as far as I gather, to appear out of the blue. One can understand its being a little difficult for her, particularly as Mark is a senior man here, and we don't wish to make any wrong moves if we can help it.'

'No, of course not. . . But I'm afraid I know very little about his friend myself.'

'Oh, dear, how irksome. Well, the thing is, Katy, Kathleen rather anticipated this and tells me she's thinking of inviting you and Tessa, along with, perhaps, Roger and his friend, whom you were with last night. Now, can I give Kathleen the hint that you might be able to come? Because I think she's rather relying upon Tessa and you to sort of get Janine circulating. I noticed she was mixing a bit last night, but it wasn't entirely up to our idea of circulating! I think Kathleen might expect her to do better than that if she had to attend many functions with Mark Hammond!'

When at last Katy replaced the telephone, after assuring Miss Munro that both Tessa and she with their escorts would be at the party, she felt very bothered. It was quite obvious Miss Munro had already perceived Janine and Mark to be having an affair of some kind, and Katy wondered if indeed Mark yet had any idea that the social set were already on the lookout for Janine as a new face and someone useful to encourage to attend charity occasions for the good of the hospital. Katy was not sure if she should alert Mark to the cautious preparations being put in hand or if she should leave everything as it was for now, especially as just at that moment the phone rang and she was told to prepare for two admissions in about an hour's time.

As it happened, the morning turned out to be far more rushed than was usual for a Sunday. Two women were admitted—one a young woman in the first stage of labour, the second woman in a bad state of advanced abortion and suffering severe bleeding.

'What's the background? Where did you find her?' Katy asked quickly in an undertone as Melanie and she helped transfer the semi-conscious woman into an operating gown and onto the bed; apparently her filthy clothes had already been stripped from her, and her body sponged down in Casualty. The woman groaned as they moved her.

'I'll go and ring for our new registrar, Bill Lodge; he's on duty today. She was apparently found lying on the side of the road. More like the sixteenth century instead of the twentieth at times, isn't it?'

'Perhaps she's a down-and-out. . .'

'Heaven only knows,' Katy said, rushing away to the phone.

In one of the small labour wards, Bill Lodge completed his examination of the woman. So far they had been able to get nothing out of her, not even her name. The registrar shook his head in despair. 'It's an inevitable abortion, I'm afraid. An early pregnancy abortion like this is often incomplete because separation of the placenta is not easy from the poorly developed perforation of the uterus lining,' he said soberly, washing his hands at the nearby basin. 'Get her into the theatre, will you, please, Sister? It has to be an evacuation of the retained products of conception. . .' He glanced at the ward clock. 'I want her down there in ten minutes.'

Katy looked down at the woman, at the cloud of curly brown hair over her pillow, her closed eyes, and the tanned regular features, beautiful in their way. And still no word issued from her lips. Katy carried on with the routine preparations. 'When was your last menstrual period, dear?' Katy asked gently, trying yet again.

The woman turned her head away on the pillow, her face suddenly in an agony of pain; she shook her head, not speaking. The porters arrived to transfer her to the theatre. Katy gave the patient's notes into Melanie's care and the woman was transported downstairs, and Katy sighed for the baby who had never really stood a chance.

In the office Tess was at the drugs cupboard. 'Dr Lodge said he might need an oxytocic drug if the blood loss is particularly heavy,' she said. 'Pethidine as well, by the look on that poor girl's face; I just happened to see her as I came in. She looks—well, sort of hippie-like; we don't see many of those these days.'

'No, that's true,' Katy said, making some notes for her report later. 'The other admission is Mrs Barclay; she hasn't gone into the second stage yet, but as far as we can tell it all seems quite straightforward. Perhaps you wouldn't mind going in to have a cheery word with her, Tess.'

'Sure. I'll just get these drugs out and everything locked away again.'

By lunchtime, Miss X, as they called her, was still sleeping, but naturally now; in the event both Tess and Melanie had had to set up a cross-matched blood transfusion for the heavy blood loss that had taken place.

Katy looked at the girl's face, which seemed younger since she had returned from the theatre, yet old before her time. 'What a tragedy,' Katy murmured. 'We know so little about people, and yet are so often with them at both birth and death.'

'That's right, it's funny how we can work for days with all the comings and goings of hospital life, and then perhaps just one admission makes us stop and think.'

'I know. By the way, Tess, if you go to lunch now, I'll follow. I want to see Joanna and I've checked that she's going for the later sitting.'

For the rest of her spell of duty that morning, although there was enough to do as well as the heavier than usual invasion of visitors—it being Sunday—Katy still could not forget the night before with Mark Hammond. On thinking about it, she was rather glad now that it was his day off. Not seeing him, much as her heart clamoured to, gave her mind the necessary space to keep a firm hold on her thoughts.

It was quite obvious now that Janine would be among them for a while longer—it was a week before the social event which Mark had hoped might see the going of her. But what the outcome of that would be Katy had no idea. Mark seemed to be in a state of permanent apprehension as to what Janine might do next, and Katy could not help sharing that apprehension in view of Miss Munro's phone call that morning.

She was still in the office when Bill Lodge rang. 'Hi, Katy, I'm just ringing to say I'll be coming up in a few minutes; I want to check the abortion case is OK. Also, is the other new patient in the second stage of labour yet?'

'No, Bill, still some way to go yet, I think. From my last examination, I would say it will be a night birth—well into the night, that is!'

'Oh, that's very considerate of her! Maybe I can snatch a few hours' sleep, then!'

'I should definitely give it a go!' Katy laughed. 'The young abortion woman is still sleeping. Incidentally, no one has made any enquiries after her. Just nothing.'

Bill Lodge gave a deep sigh. 'Well, perhaps the result, sad though it is, might be for the best, Katy. Right then, see you in a minute.'

When Katy went down for her lunch, she soon spotted Joanna's friendly wave, collected her tray of tuna salad and headed for her friend's table.

Katy had barely sat down when Joanna said, 'Hi! I wanted to hear how you enjoyed the Prof's party last night. I thought it was quite a good evening,' she said brightly. 'The grub was great too. Who was that Peter Oliver you were with? He was nice. You're a bit of a dark horse, you are, Katy Woods!'

'Excuse me, that was the first time I'd ever seen the man,' Katy laughed.

'That's what you tell me! Anyhow, any news, gossip or lies to tell me on the grapevine? Believe it or not, things were almost boring down in A and E today; I suppose it's the weather.'

'Phew, it's certainly a great day! I think Mark Hammond's the lucky one; he has today off.'

'Hey, that reminds me, someone said he was with a quite smashing girl last night at the do—it must have been after I left—but no one seems to know who she was. Do you know, Katy?'

'Well, only that she's an old friend of his, and turned up out of the blue to visit him.'

'She's not silly, is she?' Joanna giggled. 'But think what a narrow escape I had from being there with poor old Ron Green, though!'

'Rough luck, I think. I went to see him this morning. He's not too worried about his ankle, but more worried he didn't go with you last night.'

'Oh, yes, I bet.'

'I mean it. He gave me a note to give you.'

'Pull the other one, Woodsy!'

'OK. There we are!' Katy slapped the sealed envelope down on the table between them.

Joanna stared at it, and she did blush. 'You must be joking; there's nothing in it, is there?'

'Well, you could try opening it.'

Joanna took the envelope from Katy, her face deep pink as she fumbled to undo it and draw out the note.

Katy grinned. 'I'll be seeing you, then, Jo; I'll leave you to it,' she said as she stood up.

Joanna looked up from the note which she was obviously finding of some interest. 'Don't be crazy, Katy; anyone would think I was in love with the guy the way you're acting!'

'No, I must go, Jo. You take your time!' Katy laughed.

She was tired that evening as she went off duty and walked across the darkened gardens. A high wind was soughing in the trees and a slice of moon sailed through scudding clouds. In the distance she could hear the sea, and imagined the waves foaming into long, angry rollers as the incoming tide took them to the mouth of the estuary and beyond.

She shivered slightly as she went up to her room. A change in the weather always made her pensive. So often it seemed to coincide with a switch in her personal affairs. On this occasion, she thought as she went into her flat, it seemed to spell out the onset of autumn, and with that usually came floods to this part of the country. Nevertheless, once in the comfort of her domain, she soon forgot her rather sombre thoughts and indulged in the luxury of a warm bath and prepared for bed.

Even so, her mind quickly reverted to Mark Hammond and Janine and exactly what was going to transpire with regard to their strange affair. It was obvious that Mark was hell-bent on changes taking place with regard to getting Janine to return to Brunei without too much trouble, and as she listened to the gale-force wind now blowing outside it seemed to indicate trouble ahead.

CHAPTER SIX

FOR the next four days stair-rods of rain pelted down with relentless abandon. The gardens around Rosewall hung limp with the battering, all signs of summer washed away in such a short time following what had seemed endless weeks of good weather.

Nevertheless, on Fortune life went on just the same, the only difference being the streaming windows and evidence of water everywhere.

On Thursday morning, Miss X decided to discharge herself. She stood defiantly in Katy's office, telling her that she needed her outdoor clothes and intended leaving there and then.

Katy looked at the girl; her long hair was brighter and cleaner after four days with them in Rosewall, her face slightly more rounded, and yet, despite that, she appeared just as stubborn over giving any details about herself, and all she wanted was to leave.

Katy said quietly, 'I'm afraid your clothes had to be destroyed, but I expect we can find you something suitable. The social worker will be coming in about an hour; we can have a word with her to make sure she sees that you get back safely to where you're living.'

The girl's big eyes fixed on Katy as she said totally unpredictably, 'Don't worry about me, Sister. I'm on my own now. Without the baby I'll get by. My man 'as. . .' A wave of misery passed over her sun-beaten features. ''E's left me for someone else. . .' The huge eyes blurred with tears, then she said with a tremor in her voice, 'You've all been good to me 'ere. I wanted to die when I came in. 'E left me on the roadside in agony. I screamed after 'im to take me with 'im, but when 'e saw I was in trouble 'e didn't want to know. 'Ave you ever felt like killing yourself, Sister?'

The girl didn't wait for a reply, but wiped her hand across her wet eyes. 'Now I know 'e's not worth it. Curses on 'im, I say. You lot 'ave shown me what kindness is in 'ere. That's why I'm going off on me own this morning; it's time I was moving on. I want to get as far away from 'im as possible. 'E might come back to find me. If 'e did, 'e'd beat the 'ell out of me. . .'

Katy was relieved when the social worker turned up and took the poor girl under her care. They found her some fresh clothes, including a decent raincoat. The staff said goodbye, and Katy and the social worker chatted to the girl about the sort of places she might go and the names of various hostels for people like herself. Katy watched them struggle down the drive together under an umbrella, towards a small Fiat; the young woman would be given a lift, taken to a café for a warm meal, and no doubt given some money to see her on her way.

In the lift back to Fortune, Katy sighed inwardly, thinking how many tragedies in life started with close relationships, developing from love and turning thereafter, quite often, to despair. Despair was all around her in the hospital, as if she was at the very centre of people who similarly grappled with affairs of the heart that all seemed to have their darker side.

Mark Hammond was in the office when she got back. He turned from the window where he had been looking out at the forlorn scenery. 'Morning, Katy! The weather's not much to write home about, is it?' His tall, broad-shouldered presence seemed to electrify her.

'Morning, Mark! No, it's rubbish! You've been busy in the private sector these last few days, I gather.'

He heaved a sigh. 'Had time to do a lot of thinking, if that's what you mean,' he answered with a wry grin.

'I have made up my mind that the truce remains with Janine until after we have been to the Masons' dinner next week, then that's an end to it!'

Katy gave a little grin. 'Good luck to you.'

'I shall need it. Now, what's happened up here today—anything special?'

'Well, we have one patient due in this afternoon—quite straightforward, I believe. And one discharge—our Miss X went of her own accord.'

'Bill saw to her, I think.'

'Yes, that's right. Wouldn't say a word, as you know, but suddenly this morning she became quite talkative, saying that but for us she would have died. Poor young woman. Oh, her name is Melody, she's had a really rough time and is now alone to fend for herself. She hopes to make a fresh start and settle into a women's hostel somewhere.'

'Good. So long as she has a roof over her head, that's as much as we can do, I suppose.'

They talked over the night report. 'I see Mrs Stacey's had a better night. It wouldn't have been a good thing to let her go home for the weekend. You said she'd had a talk with her husband, Katy?'

'Yes, her husband will be coming in tonight so he may have better news of their daughter, Tina, but whether she'll fall in with helping her parents rather than hindering them remains to be seen.'

He shrugged. 'We can only hope.'

'Mark, would it be OK for me to have this weekend off to go home?'

'Sure, if you've cleared it with Miss Munro.'

'Yes, she says it's OK.'

'Fine. Tessa will take your place?'

'Yes, and there's another, newly qualified staff nurse who will be available to come up here if you need her.'

'Right. I'll be in this evening, then, to try and have a word with the Staceys.' He moved to the door then turned back to her again. 'You will be at the Masons' dinner next week, I hope?'

'Yes, I'll be going with Peter Oliver from Colchester.'

She thought a mere suggestion of a shadow appeared across his features. 'Oh, the blond guy you met before?'

'Yes. We got on quite well.' She didn't know why she made the remark, except that some capricious thought in her head nudged her to show Mark that she was not around solely as an adviser on his love entanglements.

'I see.' He raked her face with his eyes. 'I suppose you haven't had time to think of our next meeting? If you've remembered it, of course,' he said curtly.

She felt her hackles rise at his sudden coolness of tone. 'No, I haven't forgotten, Mark, but as I'm going home on Friday evening I was going to suggest next Monday or Tuesday evening.'

His face seemed to soften a little. 'Well. . .um. . .yes, I think Monday would suit me fine. Would seven-thirty be all right for you?'

'Sure. I'll check it with Tess, but I know she hates having an evening off on Mondays, so it would seem to be OK.'

'Right. I'll be up here this evening. Bill and one of the two new young housemen will see the admission this afternoon.'

That evening, after Katy and the sister-midwife on duty in the intensive care baby unit had checked that all was well, the babies had had their two- or three-hourly feeds, blood samples had been taken to measure gas tension, acidity and bicarbonate content, Katy could hear visitors arriving and wanted to get back to the office to answer any queries.

'Melanie,' she told the bright-eyed, auburn-haired girl before she left, 'I know Sister-Midwife would be glad of your help to watch the babies, particularly the two who are still on the Jacques catheter for feeding.'

Katy had earlier made certain that Tessa had comfortably settled the new admission in, and now she decided to check that Mrs Stacey was not getting too over-excited or worried about seeing her husband. But she need not have worried; Janet Stacey was sitting up in bed, unruly curls neatly brushed, wearing a pretty bed-jacket and just applying lipstick. 'Hi, Janet, that's the stuff; you intend knocking your husband out with the glamour tonight, then, do you?'

'What a hope, Sister, but I like to do my best!'

'Are you feeling OK?'

'Fine, considering all things.' She grinned, then her brown eyes widened as she looked at the entrance to the ward. 'Hey, look at that, Sister! It's Tina with Pete. I've never seen them so matey before!'

'There you are, my dear; let's hope it's a happy ending for you! I'll leave you now to enjoy your company, then.'

After giving a quick welcome to the two new arrivals, Katy carried on to the first-stage labour ward, where a nervous young woman was crying as she lay on the bed; then she sat up, and put her feet to the floor.

'What is it, Mrs Treen? Is there something I can get you?'

'No, thanks, Sister,' she gasped after a sudden short contraction. 'It's just that I'm worried about my little boy. My husband's taking him to my mother, and I'm so afraid he'll be crying for me.'

Katy said quietly, 'Look, give me your mother's phone number and I'll check that he's OK. Would you like me to do that?'

'Oh, yes, please, Sister.'

Five minutes later Katy was able to reassure the woman, and at the same time her husband arrived. They had a cup of tea together, and Katy left the husband carefully massaging the lumbar area of his wife's back, giving Katy the chance to see other visitors, until Tess returned from a tea-break to stay with Mrs Treen before the second stage of labour was reached.

By supper time Mrs Treen's baby had arrived; the delivery had not been too prolonged and had been quite normal, so she would most probably be going home the following day.

'Has Mrs Stacey had her visitors yet, Katy?' Mark asked after Bill had gone. 'I believe she was expecting them tonight.'

'Yes, they are here now. Her daughter turned up with Mr Stacey, and they all seem to be talking quite happily together, so perhaps things between them are improving.'

'Terrific. That's going to make a heck of a difference to Mrs Stacey. With only another couple of weeks before her baby's due, things could still go well for her.'

Katy glanced at Mark. If she was not mistaken his expression seemed somewhat preoccupied, as if something outside his hospital work was troubling him. At the same time she noted subconsciously that the wind outside was getting up again, no doubt all set for a wild night.

Mark had strolled towards the window, and was gazing out at the grey dusk that had suddenly cloaked the office with shadows. He turned from the window abruptly as she switched on the lights, saying, 'Janine has been in London for the last few days, staying with an old schoolfriend. It's been quite peaceful as far as I'm concerned, but she rang at lunchtime, saying she had to see me. God knows what it's all about.'

'Oh, it's probably some small point about the dinner party next week.'

'No, I'm afraid Janine doesn't worry too much about small points. I suppose I'll have to call in at the hotel some time this evening. It's the last thing I want to do. Neither do I wish to invite her to my flat; that would be a disaster; I'd never get rid of her!' He laughed, but

Katy knew that he wasn't really amused.

'Well,' she said quickly, 'I must get off duty now. I have to ring my mother to tell her I shall be seeing her tomorrow.'

'OK, I'll see you before you go, then, Katy.'

Once she had had her dinner and was back in her own rooms, Katy tried hard to concentrate upon her affairs after she had telephoned her mother. Nevertheless, she could not get off her mind the meeting between Mark and Janine that evening.

She closed her sitting-room windows hurriedly as a great gust of wind suddenly shook the very walls of the building; a pot of flowers she'd had on the sill toppled over, spilling blooms and water everywhere. At that same moment the telephone began to ring with irritating persistence, but by the time she had lifted the receiver whoever it was had rung off, and she went to bed.

It must have been around five the next morning, the Friday dawn light having not yet emerged, when she was wakened by, it seemed, exactly the same persistent ringing of the telephone. Sleepily, she answered it. 'Katy Woods here,' she mumbled.

'Katy, this is Miss Munro's secretary; I'm having to ring around to everyone. I have to tell you we are on a red alert at Rosewall. Will you please report at the main reception area with other members of staff, where Miss Munro must speak to you? Please come immediately.'

Wide awake now, Katy leapt out of bed and dragged on her tracksuit and trainers. Remembering to throw a raincoat round her, she ran swiftly downstairs, joined by other members of staff, all agitated by the unexpectedness of the command.

When they reached Reception from the nurses' home, several of the doctors were already at Miss Munro's side, including Mark Hammond and Bill Woods, their faces stern.

'I have had an urgent call from the combined local services,' Miss Munro was saying as they crowded into a group around her, 'warning us that excessive floods overnight, partly brought on by heavy rain recently, have, with the gales we're experiencing, caused severe breaches in the marina wall, as well as the sea-wall further towards the estuary. As you can imagine, massive damage and havoc are being wrought, but, more importantly, casualties are coming in which need to be dealt with.

'I want those of you who can, by which I mean all of you except those already on night staff, to return to your own wards now and prepare extra beds, instituting all regular emergency measures. The ambulance service is already at the marina with their paramedics, but I want medical help from housemen, and more experienced registrars to stand by to organise. . .'

The telephone on the wall behind her shrilled; swiftly she answered it, her face solemn. 'Yes, of course. Immediately. Yes, we can cope; don't worry.' Miss Munro replaced the receiver, turning to the group and saying, 'That was a message from the local police; apparently a doctor or midwife is needed for a woman who, it is thought, has just gone into labour. Unfortunately she is with her husband on board one of the small craft that has broken loose from its moorings and the gale is such that it is sweeping the boat out towards the open sea.' She glanced around anxiously. 'Mr Hammond, would you be prepared to go?'

'Of course.'

'And, as we have very little information about the case, perhaps, Sister Woods, you would go too in case your help is needed; two hands are better than one in difficult circumstances and you are used to working together.'

They agreed simultaneously just as a police van arrived outside the hospital, flashing lights reflecting on the wall. An anxious-looking policeman entered Reception, going straight to Miss Munro. 'Can we take your people down to the marina at once, ma'am? The situation is bad down there. Plenty of help's needed, that's for sure.'

'Yes, we're quite organised, Officer,' Miss Munro said immediately, making sure that Mark and Katy were supplied with all the equipment they might need for the emergency—delivery pack and portable incubator with oxygen cylinder. Then another policeman arrived, handing out oilskins, boots and protective clothing and headgear for those who could be spared to help at the scene of the disaster, while others disappeared to prepare the hospital for whatever the situation might require.

Meanwhile, in the speeding van, the two policemen tried to give Katy and Mark some idea as to how much danger the stricken craft was in. 'We don't know too much about it, Doc,' one confessed. 'Our serg just despatched us in double-quick time to get you down here. I'm told both the Sea Rescue and Lifeboat Services are standing by; in fact they are probably here already, going by the searchlights down on the shore.'

Katy was astounded at the sight when they reached the marina, water and tossing boats crashing into each other, with the fire, ambulance and police personnel busily endeavouring to put their rescue services into operation as men were being advised with their families to leave the crafts, and others, who were refusing to see their possessions float away, were being removed bodily from the water.

Even fields in the surrounding countryside were flooded; it was difficult to see where the road ended and the fields began. The sea, like a hungry monster, was now flooding up river—where the water was apparently a foot higher than usual—and winning the battle against the lorry-loads of sandbags that were being stacked against the breached walls by willing volunteers. All of this Katy and Mark witnessed while they waited for permission to board either the lifeboat or the helicopter which had landed by now a short distance away.

A burly police inspector arrived and with a friendly smile said to Mark, 'There's some doubt if it's to be a helicopter job or not, Doc. The boat out there's only an eighteen-foot motor cruiser—not very easy to winch anyone down on.' He looked at Katy with a grin. 'How are you for heights, Nurse?'

'Oh, I'm OK, thanks, Inspector, we just want to help!'

'That's the spirit, lass; bad do, though, isn't it?'

One of his men appeared at the inspector's side. 'We've just had a call, sir; it'll have to be a combined operation. Here's the captain of the lifeboat now. . .'

Katy gulped, listening to the easy banter going on around her. A moment of sheer panic suddenly seized her. Terror rose up in her throat. She would feel queasy on that angry sea. She'd sailed all her life, hadn't she? But it was different on the river. How would she ride in a lifeboat that was jumping around as if it were on a switchback, or be pulled up and down on the end of a rope to a helicopter. . . ?

Mark was at her elbow, his hand gripping her firmly, his voice urgent. 'You'll be OK, won't you, Katy? You did say you're OK sailing and all that.'

'Yes, I'll be fine, Mark,' she trilled, hardly recognising her own voice. 'No problem!'

'Attagirl!'

The captain, tanned, burly and cheery, scrunched up over the streaming pebbles after leaping ashore from his frisky craft.

'Hi, Doc, Sister! We've been in touch with Sea Rescue and they think in view of the woman's condition we should try and get her off with us first before using the 'copter. Anyway, nothing to worry about; one of us will manage it. Not much fun for her, is it? It's no wonder her husband sounded nearly demented when one of our chaps managed to receive the man's mayday call before his radio went out; good thing he sent up a red flare, otherwise we couldn't have worked so fast.'

He gave a thumbs-up sign, indicating to a member of his crew that they were about to get on board. 'Just one point, Doc—it may not be a piece of cake out there, so I suggest, if we can get aboard the little craft without the nurse, we'll do that, depending on the patient. Nevertheless, it's good that she's with us, just in case! Is that OK, do you think?'

'Anything you say, Skip,' Katy joked, feeling she was an absolute fraud at this stage in pretending she was so casual and boarded lifeboats and helicopters several times a week.

The two men gave Katy a hand into the lifeboat from the end of a jetty usually reserved for smaller craft. 'That's it, Katy; don't mind if I call you that, I hope.' The captain grinned, his calm, easy voice reaching her. 'There we are; you're on board now. Now the doc. Steady as she goes! OK, Doc? Right! We're off!'

As the engine took the boat out, they made their way towards the covered engine house to see what was going on and left all the paraphernalia of the flooding behind, the service people getting smaller and smaller, as they gathered speed and a helicopter now fluttered above them.

By the time Katy had her sea legs, any fears she'd had were past history, so absorbed was she by all the technology on board, plus the fact the captain was having a chuckle at her expense while assisting her and Mark into the unwieldy life-jackets. Giant waves were now slapping the sides of the vessel, which seemed to skim across the thunderous waves as though defying them to impede their progress.

'There she is!' someone called. 'It looks as if the

little boat's still holding together, thank God. . .'

A huge searchlight was now switched onto the floundering craft, which every now and again disappeared between deep wave-troughs, but was thrown up again. A man in a life-jacket could be seen frantically waving to them.

'Poor devil,' the captain muttered, then added, 'You OK to come on board when we can get a line across, Doc?'

'Sure,' Mark said. 'Any time you say!'

'Good man! In this gale we have to try and get in as close alongside as we can. I reckon we may have to make several tries. . .' They did, and each time the gigantic rollers thwarted them.

'We'll have to take her in astern, I think, mate!'

'OK, Captain!'

Two of the crew had a stretcher ready to hand, another was running out a lifeline to the man clinging to his precarious perch, while the captain shouted his orders against the rush of the booming sea, and the helicopter was almost comforting above. . .

One of the men was poised ready as the lifeboat was brought round rearwards. 'OK. Now!' He took one magnificent leap, landing safely on the small craft just as it dropped down into a trough. Another of the men joined him, then it was Mark's turn. Taking his instructions from the captain, on the word 'Jump!' he leapt; for a moment it seemed to Katy that he was poised in mid-air as a swell hit the lifeboat, but amazingly it helped him to land safely.

Katy was preparing herself to do the same in case there was a problem. She waited with the rest of the crew while the worried man led the group down into the flooded area. A few minutes later there was some loud shouting to attract their attention. It was Mark, now yelling through a megaphone.

'I'm afraid we have a problem!'

'What's that?' yelled the captain.

'These people are Moslems. The husband will only allow a woman doctor or midwife to see his wife. She's in a great deal of pain, but I can't convince either of them to let me see her. Can Katy come over? I don't think they're going to change their minds!'

Katy gave a thumbs-up, hearing the captain mutter, 'Oh, bloody hell.' Then he shouted, 'OK, she's coming. You stay put, Doc.'

Katy dared not look down at the heaving water as instructions were given to take the boat in as closely as possible. 'Now, love, this'll be easy,' the captain said with a cheeky grin. 'The doc will be waiting to catch you when you jump; we'll fasten this line around your waist and there'll be nothing to it! Now, when I shout, Go, leap as far as you can and the boys over there will be looking forward to giving you a hug!'

Katy's heart was in her mouth. She dared not look down at the sea. Her legs were wooden. But quite suddenly in the brilliant artificial light Mark smiled at her from the deck, both hands outstretched towards her. . . Just at that moment she heard the order, 'Go!' Automatically she went, and the next minute fell into an untidy heap on the moving deck, and Mark's arms were round her. 'Good girl!' he yelled, and Katy was aware of other male voices calling much the same thing from the comparative sturdiness of the lifeboat. The woman's husband greeted her anxiously.

'My wife, Shani. You do understand?' he said urgently as his hand took hers firmly.

'Yes. . .yes. . .' she assured him as he led her down a small, precipitous companionway, which was badly flooded, leaving Mark outside but within hearing and talking distance.

'You must be careful down here, Sister. I will guide you.' They waded cautiously into the darkness with only the man's sure touch on her hand. . .

A sudden scream and a cry of anguish rose above the roar of the wind and the crash of the sea as they entered a small cabin section, and in the light of their torches Katy could just make out the figure of a young woman lying on a top bunk, clinging frantically to the safety rail around it. Katy, by now sloshing through water up to her knees but completely absorbed by her young patient's terror, saw the woman force a brave smile following the last contraction.

'Hello, Shani! I'm Katy. Now, your husband and I are going to lift you down to the lower bunk. There, that's better.'

From a cursory examination of the girl, it was obvious she was in the second stage of labour and suffering badly from maternal distress. The girl, in her early twenties, was obviously feeling completely unable to continue in labour. Her exhaustion might have been physiological, as well as being compounded by the pain and fear she was going through. Katy pushed the girl's hair back from her face, then helped her take some painkillers.

'As soon as we get ashore, Shani, you'll be fine. . .'

'Katy. . .' She heard Mark call from outside the cabin. 'Do you need help?'

'Yes, Mark. Will you tell the captain that we're coming out now?'

At length the girl was securely belted to the stretcher. As they neared the companionway and moved up to the deck, Katy heard a voice radio to the helicopter that it would no longer be needed, that the young woman was being taken straight to hospital. The helicopter signalled its thanks, and turned to go back to base.

At that moment Mark and one of the crew fixed the stretcher to several thick hawser ropes that could withstand the small winch kept on board for such rescues. Gradually, slowly, and with great gentleness, the burden was lowered to the safety of the lifeboat, the girl's pale face half-dazed with terror and sheer joy. Next went her husband, then the rest of the crew, and, with hardly anything that could be done for the gallant little cruiser they had to leave behind, it began to break up even as they turned away towards the shore.

Mark looked mightily relieved when he told Katy that the woman was having her first child, which gave them, hopefully, a little more time. The painkillers seemed to have calmed the girl.

'It was a close thing, though,' he whispered out of hearing of both husband and wife. 'Another ten minutes and they certainly would not have been as lucky as they are at this moment.'

Katy spent the rest of the trip talking and watching over Shani, easing her worries about her baby. 'Mr Hammond will put your mind completely at rest once we get back. Seeing that your baby has decided to arrive a month early, there may be one or two things he'll have to say, but nothing for you to worry about.'

The woman smiled, then bit her lip as a further contraction gripped her.

Once they made landfall, an ambulance was waiting, and Mr and Mrs Assad were immediately whisked away to Rosewall. Katy stood watching the speeding vehicle. 'I do hope she'll be OK.'

'I'm sure she will,' Mark said thoughtfully.

Now that she was on comparatively dry land, Katy felt as if she had been away for days; in actual fact it had only been about three hours. Nevertheless, it was good to see their police inspector friend smiling at them again and offering a lift home as he congratulated them. 'Good show, both of you! Actually there's a few more of your staff waiting down the road; they've done some sterling work too, at the marina, and I think it's about time you all got back for something to eat and a bit of a rest.'

He looked up into the sky. 'We don't know yet what's

in store for us tonight; we may have to get you all out again, and even now there's a few extra patients in the hospital you didn't expect!'

The lifeboat crew gave them a great send-off, and when at last they were dropped at Rosewall Mark suggested the eight members of staff piled into his flat for drinks and a snack before going back to the hospital. They were a noisy, hilarious lot, all having done their best to help in any way they could.

Tessa and Joanna were there, even Margaret was with them, having been at home off duty from Reception, but having hurried down to the marina to offer her services to the busy Salvation Army when she'd heard of the disaster, and convinced that from then on she had served thousands of cups of tea to half the world.

'Wow! What a morning it's been already!' Joanna was saying, looking as bright as a button even though she had been on duty until ten the night before. 'I'll give you a hand in the kitchen, Mark. Come on, show me where everything is!'

All were over-excited, even mildly hysterical with the mixture of shock and stress of the occasion, but Mark was great and already producing half the contents of his freezer.

'Come on, everyone. Don't be bashful, Tess; take a few more of these sandwiches. What I'd do without this microwave I don't know, and I bought this cooked chicken for just such an occasion!'

Hilarity and relief had the crowd talking nineteen to the dozen, until eventually tiredness claimed them and gradually the group broke up and began to leave.

Margaret said goodbye to Mark, then stopped in her tracks as she went through the front door. 'Oh, I don't know if it was important, Mr Hammond—I've only just remembered. Last night some time, ages ago it seems, that lady rang—the one who rang you before—and asked if you'd call her as soon as possible.'

'OK, thanks, Margaret. I'm afraid none of us have been able to meet commitments with everything that's been going on.' He closed the door quietly, and Katy was only really aware now that the flat was suddenly very quiet and she and Mark were alone. . .

It was late morning, everything so restful—the large, comfortable room with its sage-green walls and white woodwork, thick cream carpets and deep sage-green chairs and sofas, gold tapestry curtains, and gilt reading lamps dotted about. Overall there was a tranquillity that quite belied Mark's rather derogatory remark about his flat when she'd first spoken to him on arrival. All of this was being assimilated in her mind while, as well, she experienced a secret excitement at seeing Mark's home that completely banished all thoughts of tiredness.

He had just gathered up the last of the china that they had used, and glanced at the ormulu clock on the mantle of the pale brick fireplace where an imitation coal fire flickered enticingly. Without a word, he pulled up one of the settees nearer the fire and straightened the cushions.

'Katy—' he held out his hand '—I know you must want to go, but I thought, just on this occasion, perhaps we might have a quiet chat together. We seem to have done so much since last night; honestly, when Margaret gave me that telephone message from a friend just now, for a brief second I had to stop and wonder who my friend was!' he said, laughing as she sat beside him.

'I feel rather like that myself, Mark, but I do hope Janine has not got some sort of bad news for you.'

'If it is, I don't want to know about it at this minute. I wanted to thank you for coming out in the boat this morning. You didn't have to, you know; no one would have thought any the worse of you had you refused.'

'I don't feel that I did very much, Mark.

He jerked himself up suddenly, looking into her eyes. 'Now look here, Katy Woods, all of us have to be in a permament state of readiness with our job. It doesn't fall to everyone to do the things that are noticed; nevertheless, they are necessary. Think of that chap up there in the 'copter this morning; he might have been a newly trained pilot and dying to try out his first big rescue bid. But what happened? He had to return to base without, as he may think, proving himself. That sort of thing's happening all the time.'

She leaned her sleek golden head against the back of the settee, meeting his eyes where he still sat looking into her face as if waiting to make sure that she understood what he had been trying to say. 'Thank you, Mark—yes, you have made me feel better. Perhaps there'll be another time. . .'

He gave one of those slow, enticing smiles that made her want to throw herself into his arms, as he sat visibly relaxing and sitting back staring into the fire. 'Would you believe me if I told you I have often imagined you sitting here like this with me, just talking, like the good friends that we are?' he said softly, turning his face to her again, unable to prevent himself from gazing at the eyes that had entranced him from the first moment they'd met.

She nodded, her lips curving into a delectable bow. 'Yes, Mark, I do believe you, and I certainly like to think that we are good friends.'

He took her hand, opened her fingers away from the palm, dropped a kiss on it and closed them again. 'That's a thank-you.'

The touch of his lips had sent a surge of longing through her that was beyond all reason, considering the comparatively short time she had known him. It was crazy, all those promises she had made to herself were crumbling to nothing. What was happening to her, when she could not even rely upon her own judgement? It just didn't make sense. She realised that his arm had slipped around her shoulders, the other encircling her waist. She couldn't resist. Quite suddenly it was as if some kind of destiny was working itself out in front of her very eyes. Whether it was good or bad, she was incapable of drawing back now.

His firm, cool lips brushed hers gently, then moved away; he cupped her chin in his hand, studying every beautiful curve and contour of her face before he lifted her hair from her shoulders, his long, shapely fingers running lightly through the soft, silky tresses. One hand brushed the soft pink shell-like lobe of her ear and it was the equivalent of an electric current going through the whole of her body. She tried to move from him suddenly.

'Mark, this is crazy,' she whispered. 'I think we're simply suffering a kind of reaction after what we've been doing today.' It was as if he had not heard her; his arms tightened around her and at the sudden crush of his lips against hers again she was helpless now—helpless, with a blissful feeling of wonder that elevated her entire body up to heights which she could hardly allow herself to believe.

'Katy, my darling,' he murmured, 'I've longed to do this so many times. Tell me you've felt the same. I can't think straight when you're as close to me as this, knowing that we are so right for each other. I've known it from the start.'

'Mark,' she murmured against his strong jaw, 'don't let's say things we might regret. We've been on a high this morning, it's not a normal situation.'

He clasped her even tighter. 'To hell with what's normal, Katy; we're drawn to each other; we both know that and we've tried hard to ignore it. Well, it won't go away—it can't—and that's why—' He stopped speaking suddenly because she had been running her fingers along the shapely line of his lips, brows, eyelids, back down the tense set of his jaw and along the square jut of his chin. He cried out with frustration, 'Katy, for

God's sake! What are you doing to me? You know we want each other; I love you, do you realise that? I'll say it again. I love you! Now perhaps you'll believe that I'm not just working out some kind of reaction just because you happen to be here.'

His dark blue eyes were almost black, the dark hair across his forehead emphasising the great depths she saw in them. They were full of the secrets of his life which he was prepared to share with her. In that moment of his declaration of love, she believed him. 'I believe you, my darling,' she whispered urgently. 'I think I love you too. Oh, Mark, this is like a dream from which we'll soon have to awaken.'

'No, my darling, you'll see. You'll see.' After he'd said this, their passionate kisses seemed to hold an eternal meaning. Katy was ready by now to be convinced that this had to be the lifetime's dream she had longed for, the change in her life of which she'd had a premonition a couple of weeks ago. Together now, in a daze of wonder, they walked into his bedroom, Mark taking her hand, leading her to their own paradise.

Passionately, with murmured words of love, they slowly discarded each other's clothes; it was an act of such beauty that Katy felt that she was taking part in some mystical, primitive experience in which words were an intrusion. Mark held both her hands in his; then, almost unable to bear the adoration in his eyes, she went closer to him. The fire that resulted from the contact was enough to convince them both that this was no dream but perfect, glorious reality.

He swung her up into his arms and placed her tenderly upon the bed. 'Oh, my darling, our love is going to last, I know it. Tell me it has to be the same for you.'

'Mark,' she said, her eyes sensuous in their brilliance as she met his own smouldering gaze, 'I'll say many things later but for now these moments are so special. Let's hope they are with us for always.'

His gentle hands smoothed across the velvet miracle of her skin, the shape, the female generosity of her as she lay basking in his love. Oh, God, he thought in silent fervour, please let everything be all right. Let me have her, let me love her as she deserves. I swear here and now I will make this up to her if it has to be. . .

Their consummation was more perfect than either had dared hope. His body coupled with hers in such loving surrender; they were suspended between earth and sky. The beauty and joy of their lovemaking, so natural, so uninhibited, made it feel as if they both had arrived upon a planet of love just their own—one where they could return at will and leave the rest of the world behind. Thereafter came the final bliss of two bodies as one, sated with love, sleeping in childlike innocence. The utter and complete fulfilment of a dream come true.

CHAPTER SEVEN

TO KATY, everything took on such an air of unreality that it was difficult for her to absorb all that was happening. The first thing she intended doing after leaving Mark's flat was to ring her mother and tell her about the emergency at the hospital. . .

Then with a groan she realised that just for a moment or two she had quite forgotten her mother no longer lived in Scotland and was now just a mere few miles along the coast at Clacton.

'Hi, Mum! Are you OK?' she asked brightly, once she'd got through.

'Yes, I'm fine, dear, thanks. What a time we've all had; it's been very bad here but the house is still standing! How are you? You must be tired out.'

Katy gave a wry smile. 'I am rather, Mum, yes. Afraid I won't be coming home today as planned, though. I hope to make it next week. How's Fleur?'

'Quite good really; a friend took her back to Hampstead from hospital, then she's going to bring her down here to me tomorrow. Once Ross is home from Brussels he'll stay also for a while.'

'Well, that's good, Mum. I must go, now. Just before I do, what did the doctor say about her?'

'They were very optimistic,' her mother said happily, 'so maybe things are going well at last.'

Once back on Fortune, Katy did a round of the six new pregnant patients who had been admitted for check-up and an overnight stay following the trauma they had experienced either in their boats with the flooding of the marina or with seeing their farmlands and crops under water, but so far all were expected to leave the following day.

Shani Assad had given birth to a son, Ahmed, shortly after she had been rushed into Rosewall that morning. Ahmed was now in intensive care, and she and her husband were staying in the hospital for a few days, then moving to a hotel in Maldon until they were allowed to take the baby home to London.

In the comfort of her private room, Shani, a pretty, raven-haired girl, looked at Katy gratefully. 'We shall never be able to thank you enough, Sister, for what you and Mr Hammond did. I shudder to think what the result might have been had you all arrived to save us ten minutes or so later.'

Katy smiled. 'You mustn't think of that any more, Shani; your young son needs all the attention he can get from you now. Is your husband coming back later this afternoon?'

'Yes. He has been to Maldon to see about the insurance claim for our boat. He may have to go to London about it yet, of course, but now that we are all safe it certainly makes one's priorities right. I do not think I shall ever grumble again!'

By teatime the winds were getting up once more and the state of emergency remained. Miss Munro insisted those staff who had returned from assisting that morning should be replaced by another group. Outside lights were already flickering, although the hospital had its own generators for electricity; also care and prudence had to be shown with regard to medical supplies while transport was difficult.

Katy was busily checking the drugs cupboard when there was a tap on the door and Mark came striding in, white coat over an immaculate light grey suit, a lilt in his walk, eyes bright when he looked at her. 'Hi, Katy, I wondered if there was any tea going spare?'

She grinned, picking up the phone. 'No, but I'll see

what I can do. Can I have tea for Mr Hammond?' she added, speaking into the receiver. 'For two, please, yes.'

When they were settled with a tastefully arranged tea-tray, including a plate of biscuits, Katy's eyes widened. 'Wow! What it is to be a man! I wouldn't have received such treatment.'

He grinned. 'Katy, just pour the tea and get on with it, please,' he teased. 'From now on I'm going to be exceedingly strict with you. . .as I was being this morning, for instance!'

She blushed charmingly. 'Really, Mr Hammond! Although seriously, Mark, I can hardly believe any of it is true on thinking back now.'

He poured the tea, handing a cup to her with a loving grin. 'I can assure you it is absolutely true, Katy,' he said softly, 'and I want to tell everybody!'

'For heaven's sake, not yet! Anyway, we need to talk to each other; suddenly there seems so much to say.'

A small frown eclipsed the happiness on his features. 'Afraid there is. I had a call from Janine earlier, and again she says she has something very important to say to me at the hotel but refuses to tell me what it is until we meet. I said whilst the emergency was in place I could not possibly leave here. So, as she slammed the phone down on me, I imagine she was not too pleased! However, Katy—' he had been leaning his long back against the radiator, but took a step towards where she was sitting at her desk and briefly caressed the side of her cheek, glancing up at the clock '—as we're virtually on call if more staff are needed out there tonight, I wondered if we should meet for a little while at my flat tonight, or yours if you prefer, just to have a drink together?'

'Great idea,' she said, but added, 'Perhaps it should be your place. You know what we said about gossip.'

'Right! Fine! About nine OK?'

'Yes, sure.'

Katy closed the drugs-cupboard door, a small furrow on her brow, saying thoughtfully, 'I wonder what Janine has to say that's so terribly urgent?'

As he made towards the door, Mark raised his eyebrows, then smiled at her. 'My dear Katy, nobody ever really knows what Janine cooks up in that head of hers. I'm afraid I'm in no hurry to know either. See you later, then.'

When he had gone, Katy went across to the staff cloakroom to wash her hands, and, on leaving, saw the back view of Janet Stacey's tall figure in her dressing gown just leaving one of the bathrooms. Katy was about to return to her office to make notes for her day report when she saw Janet stumble against the wall, and heard her give a low moan. . . Swiftly, Katy was at her side.

'Janet, what's wrong? Come along, dear; let me help you back to bed.'

'It's OK, Sister; I suddenly felt sick and vomited slightly back there. I have a bad headache too with flashing lights. I don't know what's the matter with me. . .'

Katy beckoned to Melanie, who was helping Sandra with the bed-making—rather more of it that day with the new admissions resting in bed. 'Give me a hand, please, Melanie; we must get Mrs Stacey back into bed.'

A few minutes later the woman flopped back on the pillows, looking pale and ill. 'Stay with Mrs Stacey; I'll ring Mr Hammond right away.'

When Mark returned to the ward after being paged from the private sector, Katy went with him to the woman's bedside, drawing the curtains closed behind her.

Mark smiled. 'Hi, Mrs Stacey. Now, the one thing you must not do is worry; we're simply going to be extra careful because we don't need any set-backs at this stage, do we? I want further tests to be carried out, like placental function, cardiotocograms and ultrasound scan. . .' While speaking he examined Janet's abdomen briefly. He turned to Katy. 'Sister, I want to have Mrs Stacey down in the theatre for a thorough check, particularly as there has been some slight bleeding.'

Tears filled Janet's eyes. 'You don't think this means the baby's in trouble after all this, do you, Mr Hammond?'

Mark shook his head firmly. 'No, I don't want you to start thinking along those lines; we're just being cautious, Mrs Stacey. Now, I'll see you downstairs in half an hour, right?' He patted her head comfortingly.

'OK.' Janet was dabbing her nose and eyes.

Katy squeezed her hand. 'Janet, everything's going to be all right, you'll see.'

In the office Mark Hammond was going through Mrs Stacey's notes. 'She's forty-three, isn't she. . . ?' he mused. 'I'm not going to allow this bleeding to continue. As you know, she may well be losing more blood than is obvious and of course with pre-eclampsia that's a distinct possibility; the blood pressure may have been normal but there're now other signs of shock like headache, flashing lights and vomiting. We need to set up an intravenous infusion of blood and monitor the central venous pressure. We must replace the blood loss; about one litre would be normal in this case.'

'Yes, right,' Katy murmured.

'Oh, and we'll carry out a coagulation screen and correct the defects. I'll see you downstairs with Mrs Stacey, Katy. I think it's best that you're there; someone familiar will make her feel better. Perhaps you would ring and tell her husband that I'd like to see him in about an hour's time if he can manage it; I believe he runs a small grocery shop near here so he should be able to.'

'You think the baby will have to be induced, then, if not a Caesarean. . . ?'

Mark turned towards the door. 'I'm afraid it's looking

that way.' He flicked his head suddenly with a hand. 'Oh, yes, and will you organise fresh frozen plasma to alternate with whole fresh blood, cross-matched, for the possibility of coagulapathy occurring suddenly; prevention's better than cure.' He glanced at his notes again. 'That's it, I think, and there's a prescription on your desk for Omnopon which, apart from helping Mrs Stacey's pain, will allay some of her anxiety.'

Two hours later when Janet Stacey was back from the theatre, Mark Hammond returned to her bedside to discuss with her and her husband what was to happen on the strength of his findings. Katy accompanied them while Mark explained carefully what he wanted to do.

'The result of my examination, Mr Stacey, is that, provided your wife and baby are in the right state, which I believe they are, I have to consider the induction of labour. The greater risk of eclampsia—if pregnancy is allowed to continue—must be balanced against the risk of prematurity if induction is carried out too early, and as your wife has now gone almost full term I consider the induction or, if necessary, a Caesarean to be the more satisfactory decision. I should like to get it started tomorrow morning at nine. I will, of course, discuss it with my registrar, Dr Lodge, and you may rest assured our concern is only for your wife and baby.'

'But Janet—will it be best for her?' the man queried anxiously.

'Yes, Mr Stacey, in my opinion it will be best for them both. I'll be able to say more tomorrow. I've just given you the options and that's as far as I can go at the moment.'

Mark and Katy left the husband and wife talking. Janet Stacey was a practical woman and they both knew that she and her husband would accept what her consultant had advised.

* * *

In Mark's flat much later that evening, Katy sat with him, talking shop for a while until he said suddenly, 'Katy, you do believe everything I said this morning, that I truly love you?'

Her smile was radiant. 'I want to believe it more than anything in the world, Mark, but. . .but. . .it all seems so. . .so dream-like.'

He took her hand in his as they sat together on the couch in the comfortable room. 'Dreams do come true sometimes, my darling. . .' They kissed, and for a while were both swept away in a world of their own. Adoringly, he touched her hair, running a tender hand along the side of her face. 'You are beautiful, Katy; I shall never cease to tell you.'

She took one of his hands in hers, his long, slender fingers so strong, so artistic, the nails beautifully manicured, and intertwined her fingers with his, and leaned her cheek against them. 'Such a simple touch, Mark, but the contact is sending mad, wild messages!'

He chuckled, kissing her lovingly on the tip of her short, straight nose. 'Sweetheart, I certainly know what it's doing to me!' He grinned. 'I think I'll go and make us some coffee. You said you didn't want a drink, didn't you?'

'No, thanks, Mark. . .'

She admired him as he strode out to the kitchen, then joined him, leaning leisurely against the doorframe while he switched on the coffee. He glanced up at her, that small tilted smile of his lips as always going straight to her heart. She waited until the tray was ready, and they both went back to the sitting room, indulging in pointless hospital gossip, their laughter happy and confident as together they sat down, he with his arm around her shoulders, the close proximity causing them to forget the coffee for the next five minutes.

'Hey,' he said, 'I'm failing in my duties, Katy.' He poured and handed her a cup. 'Sugar, cream?'

'Neither, thanks.'

'Nor me.' He grinned.

She stared into her coffee for a few moments then said quickly, 'Mark, what's happening about Janine now?'

'Well, she knows we're all on more or less permanent call here at Rosewall, and she cannot jam up our switchboard with her concerns. That's about all there is, really.'

'I see. . .yes,' she said thoughtfully. 'By the way, Mark, I said I was going to tell you about my ill-fated marriage. I did promise, and you have told me about Janine yourself.'

'Well, I wanted to leave it to you, Katy, but I must say I think so much about you that I want to hear everything. You can begin with how much you weighed as a baby if you like!'

She giggled. 'No, I don't think I'll go that far back!'

She started to tell him how she had first met Steve on the train home to Scotland, and of the immediate rapport they'd had between them, how they had married within three months and come south to work.

'He had bought a small house in Basingstoke for us,' she told him quietly. 'The thriving engineering firm he owned did well enough for us not to have any money problems. We were happy. He often had to go away to the Continent on business. I hated it when he went: sometimes it was for a week, a fortnight, but I became used to it. Even so once he was back home each time it was like a second honeymoon, and there were presents.'

Then she hesitated slightly and Mark saw the pain in her eyes, and, placing his hands upon hers, gently said, 'Katy, I don't want you to continue if it hurts like this. . .'

She sat up straight, no longer leaning against his shoulder, her mind distant. She continued, as if he hadn't spoken. 'Then came the day I received the first of the anonymous letters. Hideously uninformative and yet with a threatening tone, sent from somewhere in France. A woman's handwriting simply asking if I really knew my husband, Steve. . .

'I was deeply shocked. At first I thought it was some sort of hoax, then after hours of anguish I couldn't ignore the fact that the. . .the. . .person had used my husband's name, and had found my address. After a terrible night of uncertainty I decided it might just be one of those poor demented creatures who had found us in the telephone directory.'

She looked at Mark suddenly, her eyes sad yet beautiful in the mellow lamplight, almost as if she had forgotten he was there, then smiled. 'Oh, Mark, it's so lovely to be with you. . .' For a while he held her close in his arms and that was all she needed—just the comfort of this man who she knew in her heart so truly loved her. . .

She carried on. 'At first I said nothing to Steve—I didn't want to worry him—but then came another three letters, but by that time I was nearly beside myself with shock, so I rang Steve. He was great. While he was home two more letters arrived telling me that the woman was Steve's legal wife. She had their child, and was coming to London.'

Katy bit her lip, trying to stop the tears, but Mark rocked her gently in his arms, and it was impossible. 'Oh, Mark, I feel such an idiot acting this way, but honestly it's the first time I've ever talked to anyone outside the family; it must sound so. . .so. . .'

'Absolutely terrible, Katy. The trauma of such a thing for you must have been horrendous. Oh, my dear. . .' He brushed a long strand of hair from her face. 'Katy, don't tell me any more, please; I hate to see you suffering like this. . .' He handed her a folded handkerchief from his pocket.

Katy smiled, dabbing her eyes, loving his tenderness.

'No, I'm OK really, Mark; I'll just make the rest brief.' She told him then of her brother Ross's help and how the anonymous letters were traced. The wife agreed to go to court with them, and ultimately Steve, after serving the sentence meted out to him, returned to his wife and child and they now lived in South Africa.

As she finished speaking, Mark was shaking his head in disbelief. 'Katy, my darling, I hardly know what to say; it's no wonder that you've been cautious and, if I might express it this way, somewhat withdrawn at times. It's a most terrible burden that you've had to carry. I don't know how you have managed that cool, calm exterior; it's incredible.'

She was smiling now, shaking her head, the quietly happy expression on her face revealing the intense relief she felt at being able to confide so much to Mark, who himself knew what miseries love could bring. 'No, Mark, I'm not so very different to anyone else. We all handle things in our own way. . .' She took a deep sigh. 'I'm only so very glad that I have been able to talk to you in this way; it's so easy to do, I realise that now. I can well understand why Janine found you ready to listen to all her various reasons for falling in and out of love. . .'

He was about to answer when the telephone rang. Mark picked up the receiver at his side. 'Damn,' he muttered, 'I bet it's the hospital. Yes? Hammond speaking. Yes. I see. Get the ambulance to pick me up on its way to the marina, then, will you, please? I shall be outside my flat.'

He sighed, putting the phone down. 'Sorry, darling, that's it, I'm afraid. A woman has gone into labour in one of the cottages in the flooded area; they've been working to save some of their belongings and now the wife is in a bad way. I must go.'

'Should I come with you?'

'No, Katy, you're still on call too; they might need

you here. Even though the floods are dying down, there are still casualties coming in. If you do have to go out on call, just look after yourself.'

He kissed her as a ring came at the door. 'Bye, see you later.'

Katy returned to her room, but was not called out that night, for which she was grateful.

Next morning at breakfast Miss Munro thanked them all for their work and said that she had been told officially that the red alert was no longer in place for the hospital. 'But of course,' she added, 'we still have extra patients, and there may yet be more with the aftermath such weather conditions bring.'

Joanna, who was at Katy's table, finished her breakfast, looking sceptical. 'She doesn't sound very cheerful; maybe there're more storms on the way.'

Katy toyed with her toast dreamily. 'We shall have to deal with it as it comes, I suppose. All I know is we've quite a busy session on the ward today.'

Joanna was observing Katy closely as she spoke, and couldn't quite make out what it was about her that seemed different that morning. 'I say, Katy,' she remarked quizzically, 'no one should look as good as you do at seven in the morning! I've never seen you so. . .so—well, for want of a better word, radiant. . .'

Katy had the grace to blush, and stumbled over her reply. 'Really? It must just be one of my lucky days!'

Joanna grinned. 'You're a dark horse! I think you are holding something back. . .something really exciting!'

Katy finished her coffee. 'Hey, talking of such things, you never told me about the letter I gave you from Ron Green; was that exciting?'

'Nothing like changing the subject! Exciting? You must be joking! I wouldn't call a cup of coffee in the staff rest room madly exciting, would you?'

'Oh, I don't know, it depends what you were talking about!'

'Do me a favour, Katy; even though he's in plaster I still think he's a big-head!' She stood up, pushing her chair back. 'But, just for the record, I did find him fairly interesting, even though I still think he's a big-head!'

'I thought you were going to tell me he's a completely different man once you get to know him.'

'I haven't noticed it to that extent—yet!'

Fortune, that Saturday morning, was busy as Katy had predicted. Mark Hammond's discussion with Mr and Mrs Stacey had led to the couple's agreeing with Mark that their child be delivered that day by induction of labour. Katy went to Janet's bedside. 'Morning, Janet, this is your big day! Did you sleep last night?'

'Yes thanks, Sister; I was quite surprised myself.'

'Sheer relief, I expect. Now, Night Sister made sure you didn't have any breakfast, I hope. As Mr Hammond explained, there may be no need for a general anaesthetic, but this is just in case.'

'Oh, that's been looked after; I couldn't eat a thing anyway. I hope they're all right at home. Our girl, Tina, called in just before Pete left last night. Honestly, Sister, I can't believe she's the same person since Pete and I had that long talk with her. I know she'll be here later today, she told us she can hardly wait to see the baby.'

'Oh, that's tremendous news, Janet; I'm sure everything will be fine from now on.'

Mark arrived just after the night staff had left, the smile he gave Katy convincing her that, loving him as she did, admiring the tall elegance of him, the inner strength she knew he possessed, she was full to overflowing with happiness.

'Morning Katy! Did you have to go out last night?'

She smiled at his thoughtfulness. 'No, Mark, and Miss Munro has already pronounced the hospital off the red alert for the present.'

'Good, I didn't get back until four this morning so some time today I intend catching up with some sleep.' He picked up Janet Stacey's papers that were lying on her desk for him. 'Now, let's see; I want to give Mrs Stacey intravaginal prostaglandin in a pessary. Initial conservative dosage of 2.5 milligrams to facilitate amniotomy. As she's had three children that should start things going. We'll go along and see her, I think.'

Tessa tapped on the office door, popping her head round it. 'Excuse me, Mr Hammond, Dr Lodge has been delayed by traffic on his way back from Dover, but he should be here within the hour.'

'Oh, that's fine; thanks, Staff.'

Together, Mark and Katy went into the ward. 'Hello, Mrs Stacey, all hale and hearty, I hope!'

'Morning, Mr Hammond, I can hardly wait!'

'That's great. Well, we're going to give you a pessary. That should begin the induction. Now, I don't want you to worry; for parents like yourself, who have already had several children, the dosage we're giving initiates labour in more than fifty per cent of patients now that the baby's at term. I want you to just relax; we'll be keeping an eye on you. If by any chance the cervical response is not satisfactory we'll repeat the therapy after about four to six hours, or reassess the need for induction. But I have a feeling that we're not going to be waiting that long!'

He examined Janet's abdomen gently, saying to Katy, 'I shall want recordings of the maternal and foetal heart rate and the maternal heart rate from the start of labour. Mrs Stacey, we did check that you haven't got asthma or allergies to the drug? That's right, isn't it?'

'Yes.'

'Good. I shall see you later, then.' He smiled encouragingly, saying in an aside to Katy, 'We'll keep a watchful eye on Mrs Stacey; close observation of both mother and foetus is essential. We don't want to invite any complications,' he added, and they did the rest of the round together, mainly having a word with patients brought in during the flood, now hoping to be discharged.

Four hours later to Katy's relief Janet went into labour and was removed to the labour ward where both Bill Lodge and Mark Hammond examined her, both satisfied with the cervical action so far. When Bill Lodge had gone, Mark Hammond had allowed Melanie, the keenly intelligent first-year nurse, to be present while he explained gently to Janet how the present situation could change.

'You see, Mrs Stacey, induction of labour must be governed by strict criteria. You, as the patient, will accept the situation better if you understand the reason for the interference. Induced labour often appears longer, because the total duration is contained in the labour ward. Nevertheless, if you require assistance with delivery because of foetal distress, there will be no delay of any kind.'

Janet nodded with a smile. 'I'm OK, Mr Hammond; I think you're more worried than I am!'

'Good girl...' He patted her hand. 'It shouldn't be too long now. So far, so good.'

By teatime late that afternoon Janet surprised and pleased them all by giving birth to a 3.34 kilogram daughter, with a mass of dark hair like her mother. Pete Stacey had been with his wife throughout, and now, with a gasp of joy, Janet held out her arms for the baby, both she and her husband in tears when they looked at the child's tiny features and perfectly formed little body. Still drowsy after the analgesic inhalations she had had, Janet nevertheless was triumphant and peaceful after waiting for so long. 'Thank you, Sister, Mr Hammond. Thank you.'

Once the paediatrician had taken the baby for checks, normal routine was carried out, and Janet was soon back in bed in the ward, proud as Punch. Her husband was there, and daughter Tina, all now enjoying a cup of tea together. Katy returned to the office to attend to the paperwork, and half an hour later Mark joined her, looking less buoyant than he had when they were in the labour ward.

'Katy, do you know what tomorrow is?' he asked quietly.

Katy looked up from her writing. 'No, I've no idea!'

He nodded. 'Well, I suppose with all that's been going on we might both be forgiven—'

'What is it, Mark?'

He pushed a slim hand through his hair. 'It's Professor and Mrs Mason's dinner party.'

Katy's long-lashed eyes widened. 'Oh, heavens! It had gone from my head completely, Mark. . . What are we going to do? I feel so unprepared; I mean, I haven't contacted anyone else within the last day or two and Tess hasn't said a word.'

'Not to worry; it must still be on, otherwise we would have heard before now. I'm going downstairs; I'll ring the Masons and call you back.'

Katy discussed it with Tess, who seemed quite undeterred. 'Don't worry, Katy. Roger said the other night that Peter Oliver had chatted to him about it, so it's obviously still on.'

Tessa glanced at her friend after checking the medicine trolley for the baby unit. 'You seem to be unduly worried about it, Katy?'

'Not really. I suppose I was thinking of Mark's friend, Janine; she was apparently very put out that she couldn't contact him during the alert.'

Tessa shrugged. 'Too bad. . . Do you feel like going down for a cup of tea before me? You look as if you could do with one!'

Downstairs, Katy wondered as she drank her tea what Tessa was truly thinking. If she had an inkling of the new closeness between her and Mark, she obviously would not say.

With Janine giving the impression that Mark was solely her property it was rather difficult. Nothing could be further from the truth. Mark seemed dead set on making this dinner engagement the last that Janine would share with the hospital people before going back to where she came from.

There was no doubt she was a woman of very complex ideas, but Katy had no worries regarding Mark since they had declared their love for each other. She was longing to make it public knowledge, but Mark wanted to be shot of Janine first, which was understandable.

She had just returned from doing her last round of the ward that evening, having had a happy conversation with the Staceys and their daughter, Tina—the entire family appeared to be reunited by the arrival of the new baby—when she heard her telephone ringing. It was Mark.

'Katy, Mark here. Everything's still OK for tomorrow evening. I've also rung to remind Janine; she hadn't forgotten. She seemed rather over-excited on the phone, although she didn't repeat the fact that she had something to tell me so perhaps it's not as important as you thought!'

'Thanks for letting me know, Mark; I'll see you tomorrow, then. I think an early night's necessary for us both, don't you?'

'Definitely. . . Sleep tight, my darling.'

CHAPTER EIGHT

THE dinner party at Rupert and Kathleen Mason's home was well under way. Napery and silver gleamed amidst bowls of Kathleen's favourite white blooms, highlighted by masses of dark green foliage which matched the bottle-green and white interior of the long, narrow dining room, where guests were by now enjoying one of the mouth-watering desserts that Kathleen insisted upon making herself.

She laughed in answer to Mark's question. 'Yes, Mark, having brought up our four daughters with voracious appetites, I'm afraid I just can't break the habit now!'

Rupert Mason glanced at his wife lovingly. 'My dear, you're being too modest as usual. Mark, believe me, I am just as bad as the girls over Kathleen's cooking; I certainly understand why they are not too interested in leaving home! It's a good job they are not with us tonight, otherwise they'd have a lot more to say!'

Katy and Mark smiled across the table at each other, seated as they were around a long, U-shaped one.

When coffee was served, everyone elected to remain where they were, especially as by now conversation flowed and was helped along by a delicious apricot liqueur. Kathleen chuckled and told them they had brought it back from a Spanish holiday. 'We think it's delicious.' She smiled. 'Very gentle on the stomach! I remember once when we were in Germany. . .'

Convivial conversation, both interesting and amusing, went back and forth amongst them all.

Peter Oliver, seated at Katy's side, set down his liqueur glass with a smile, saying, 'You know,

Kathleen mentioned just now about Spain; as yet it's a country I have never visited. . .'

As he spoke, his eyes held hers, full of admiration, perhaps for the black dress she was wearing for the second time at the Masons'. Mark had been so fulsome then in his praise of the way she'd looked. Even now, with Janine chattering loudly at his side to all and sundry, from time to time Mark's dark gaze would lock with hers, and all she could think of was that this wonderfully charismatic man was in love with her, and she with him. . .

Peter's pleasant voice continued. 'What about you, Katy, have you ever been there?'

'Um. . .yes, I have as a matter of fact. Only to the north of Spain. We stayed in the Pyrenees a few kilometres from the French border, where we used to cycle to the local patisserie for their gorgeous cakes with our mid-morning coffee!'

He laughed. 'Maybe that's why you used a bicycle—to appease your conscience!'

'Well, whatever it was, it worked—I hope.' She grinned, glancing down at her enviable figure.

Just then, the guests began moving into the large drawing room from where light music drifted, and several couples, including the Masons, began to dance.

Peter smiled at Katy. 'We'll join the others, shall we?' he asked.

Katy hardly heard him, for at that moment she became very anxious for Mark. He was looking embarrassed at Janine's sudden antics as she left the table, clasping his arm, gazing up into his eyes, whispering into his ear, then giggling skittishly, saying, 'Oh, sweetie, let's dance; I do love you.' Her voice was getting louder and louder as the alcohol, of which she'd had more than was sensible, against Mark's advice, took over.

For the next hour the party gathered momentum, until

someone asked Tess to give a vocal rendering of one of the love songs from a current London musical. 'No, I'm no good when it's this sort of gathering,' she protested. 'Am I, Roger?'

He grinned. 'I haven't had the pleasure yet, Tess, and where else do you sing if not at gatherings?'

Tessa giggled. 'In the bath! But you know what I mean—friends, relatives. It's different somehow!'

The crowd insisted, and when Tessa's beautiful, clear but husky-toned voice filled the room it held the crowd spellbound. When the final note died away, there was utter silence, and then genuine applause broke out as she was showered with well-deserved praise.

At the same time, Janine appeared at Katy's elbow, Mark a little way behind. 'Now,' Janine said, her voice shrill, 'I'd like to make an announcement before we go any further. . .' She thrust herself forward, the guests out of curiosity closing around her.

'Wow!' someone called from the back of the room. 'We didn't know it was going to be talent night!'

'It isn't,' Janine called. 'You see, I just want you all, as my friends here tonight—' her voice slurred as she swayed slightly against Katy, then righted herself '—to listen to something special I want to share with you, because I am so happy!' She shook her head as if unable to control it, then stopped when she realised Mark was at her side trying to dissuade her from whatever it was she intended saying. She shrugged off his arm. 'No, darling, I'm going to tell them; why should we keep it a secret any longer. . .?'

At the words, Katy felt her heart lurch. A sudden chill gripped her. A stultifying numbness was waiting to consume everything that was warm, glowing and loving within her. She was only capable now of moving as if on puppet strings, yet too well aware of the silly, inebriated voice carrying on. . .

'Anyway, I expect you to believe me. . .' Janine gave one of her little-girl pouts.

The voice from the back rose again. 'Get on with it then, Janine; we're all ears!'

Amidst good-humoured laughter, she smiled sweetly, turning to Mark, looking up into his face with maudlin adoration. 'What I wanted to say at this lovely party is that Mark. . .' she slid an arm around his waist when he moved forward as if to restrain her '. . .is my super husband.' She paused, as if knowing the impact her words would make.

A gasp went round the room; one or two people rallied and gave smiling congratulations, others just seemed too taken aback to say anything. Mark had never mentioned a wife. . .

Then, as if the words had penetrated suddenly, noisy best wishes broke out.

'Well done, Mark!'

'Bit of a dark horse, I'd say!'

'Two dark horses, I'd say!'

'May we know how long you've been spliced?'

Janine stepped forward, by now thoroughly revelling in the attention she was receiving. 'Thank you, everyone, from us both!'

But Mark's authoritative voice suddenly changed the atmosphere from one of light amusement to barely concealed anger. 'I think I had better get you back to the hotel, Janine, now. Come along, you've had your fun; we're leaving this instant!'

Janine flopped a limp hand onto his shoulder. 'Mark, don't be such a spoilsport! I was just beginning to enjoy myself. I wanted everyone to know about us. . .'

A nerve jerked in Mark's temple as he tried to keep control of the situation. 'Some other time, I'm afraid,' he told her with a forced smile. 'We must say a quick goodnight to everyone now, and be on our way. . .'

But Janine stood her ground. 'You see how masterful

he is with me! That's why I love him so much.' She swayed as Mark attempted to move her bodily. He was damned if he was going to allow Janine to make an exhibition of herself any more than he could help, but she had moved from him slightly.

'Janine, we are going. . .*now*!'

'Well, I am not!' she flung at him, her voice suddenly losing the treacly tones she had been using. 'I want to tell our friends one more thing! You want to hear it, don't you?' She had raised her voice as if addressing a crowd of hundreds. Mark's hold on her arm now was like a vice, but she ignored it.

A few voices called, 'Yes.'

'OK! Well, guess what? Mark and I have hit the jackpot! I'm pregnant! Isn't that tremendous, darling? There's no need for you to look like that. It's a surprise. I wanted to keep it as a special announcement for tonight! When I first knew, I got on the phone to you because I simply had to tell you, but you were busy all the time with the floods, so then I decided that this couldn't be a better occasion amongst our friends!'

Katy was conscious of Tess at her elbow, while Roger and Peter made off to collect some refreshments that Kathleen, always the soul of diplomacy, had suddenly announced were now laid out in the dining room. As soon as Mark and Janine had left, music concealed the wave of gossip, until gradually it receded and people began to act more normally, then subsequently they began to take their leave in ones and twos, giving the impression that nothing untoward had happened to mar the party.

Katy remembered little more of that terrible evening. She only knew that Tess was beside her still, the men having gone to Roger's flat for a drink. The two girls went up to Katy's rooms, Tess making her a milky drink while she sat on the arm of a chair staring into space.

Tess looked anxious. 'Katy, dear, you look so pale.

Are you sure it's just that liqueur you had; I mean the rest of us seem to be OK. Except for that stupid Janine, of course, but she's something different altogether!'

The name seemed to bring Katy out of the daze she was in. Sipping her drink, she said quietly, 'It's nothing to worry about, Tess. I'm just tired, I think; we've all had a stressful few days recently, haven't we?'

Tessa studied her friend, the black dress, in which she had looked so radiant only a few hours before, had now drawn all colour and animation from her face. 'Are you sure there's nothing I can get you, Woodsy? You were so good to me when I was desperate about Roger. I want to be of some use to you.'

'You are, Tess, believe me. By the way, how are you and Roger getting on?' Katy thought her voice seemed to come from a long way off.

A beautiful smile spread over Tessa's face. 'We couldn't be happier really, Katy.' Then a small frown creased her brow. 'But, the only thing is, Helen hasn't been too good these last two weeks, and there's a possibility that she may have to go into hospital for an observation period.'

'Oh, I'm sorry, Tess. I suppose there's not a great deal you can do to help really, is there?'

Tessa looked pensive. 'Only try to appease a deep-seated guilt, but that's something I still have to come to terms with. I can't bear to face the ultimate decision, though. . .'

Katy smiled, with a wry serenity. 'You and Roger will work out whatever's best. So long as you're both of the same mind, that's the main thing.'

Tessa nodded absently. 'You know, Katy, I was just thinking then of Mark Hammond; I cannot believe he's been married to Janine on the quiet all the time he's worked here. Hell, if he were my husband, I wouldn't expect him to tuck me away out of sight, would you?'

'No, I wouldn't,' Katy said, finishing her drink. 'But

Janine must be telling the truth, I suppose—that she's married and having a baby.'

Tessa looked perplexed. 'Well, she made it pretty public, didn't she? But I think there's something funny with that woman. It doesn't seem to me like a normal relationship.' She glanced at her wrist-watch. 'Oh, Lord, it's nearly midnight. Sorry, I've kept you talking, Katy; I'll get back to my quarters now, after I've rung Roger at his flat and said we're both flaked out. They'll understand.'

'Don't worry, Tess; I've been so glad of your company.'

'Are you sure you're feeling better now?'

'Absolutely, thanks. I know it's a funny thing to say, but I suddenly feel more like my old self as I was a few weeks ago before Mark Hammond changed everything.' Her brain hammered.

'I get your meaning, Katy. That to me sounds like a large hint about the way old Mark Hammond's been working you since he arrived. You know, I should think all of that could be because, with Janine on his mind, it's enough to send him round the bend. On the other hand that's no reason why his private worries should be inflicted upon you, is it?'

'I hadn't thought of it that way, Tess, but you could be right. If anyone, I felt sorry for the Masons tonight; it must have come as quite a shock to them having Janine throwing such a bombshell into the assembled company as she did.'

'You can say that again. But they're such a nice level-headed couple. I shouldn't think it upset them too badly. They seem to like Mark Hammond, and no doubt will continue doing so.' Tess picked up her handbag and jacket. 'Now, are you quite sure there's nothing else I can get you, Katy?'

'No, absolutely nothing, thanks, Tess. I'm going

straight to bed now, you've been great tonight—I do appreciate it.'

'I've done nothing, and, don't forget, we can manage if you don't feel like coming on duty tomorrow.'

When the door closed on Tessa, Katy remained seated, her headache lessening a little since taking the painkillers. The evening had been a horrendous disaster.

Eventually she stirred herself, automatically doing all the usual things she normally did when getting ready for bed, including turning on the radio to check that her watch was correct. She must have been a minute or so earlier than usual because unexpectedly the melting notes of a romantic love song drifted into the room. Immediately she recalled hearing exactly the same one when she and Mark had had dinner together that night on the river. . .

Tears—the sort that just happened without warning—welled up into her eyes as she snapped off the radio, not caring now whether her watch was fast or slow. As she blew her nose, all she knew was that once again she had made an utter fool of herself. . .

She was in bed when the telephone rang, and thought it probable that it was Tess. Instead it was Mark, his voice urgent. 'Katy, I must speak to you!'

About to put the phone down, she heard him draw in a breath and say quickly, 'No, please don't cut me off. At least let me tell you how very sorry I am about tonight. I must explain—'

'There's nothing to explain, Mark.'

'Look, Katy, there's a lot to explain, and I intend doing it.'

'I'm sorry, I have to be on an early shift tomorrow. Goodnight, Mark.' She replaced the receiver, hands shaking, heart pounding, her mind in far too much of a whirl to listen to what he had to say even if she wanted to. It was all over between them anyway. Now, she must begin to rebuild her life again instead of imagining impossible dreams with a man who, it had seemed, offered her everything. She realised too late now that it was nothing but a rerun of the stark experience she had only so recently endured with Steve.

Katy knew, as tiredness and exhaustion swept over her, that in the morning in the cold light of day her suffering would really begin. But for now she would shut herself away from life's realities and sleep; the numbness that had seized her earlier would see her through the night.

Next morning as Katy opened her eyes despair was waiting. It was exactly as it had been before—the bitterness, the shattered pride, the Stygian gloom she now had to enter each day while pretending nothing was wrong. She got up, showered and dressed mechanically, put away her clothes from the night before, then tidied the flat.

Flinging her navy cloak around her, she went out into the still, calm morning, amazed that the autumn nip in the air at least made her feel she was alive and not now encased in that terrible blackness of shock which sapped her every thought. Come to think of it, she would not allow it to happen again, she told herself as she crossed the grounds.

Vaguely she noticed thin layers of white mist streaked above the flower beds, late roses hung about with cobweb necklaces that shone like diamonds in the rising sun. In fact, quite suddenly, Katy experienced an intense feeling of incredulity that her life had again taken such a terrible turn, almost as if she had been drawn back into the past.

Yet, still the beauty around her was there, unsullied and unspoilt despite the drama of the floods. Rather like herself, it had been swamped by a floodtide of events bringing such misery, but the world still went on despite the devastation wrought, and miraculously, in front of her eyes, was already the beginning of recovery as each day passed. . . So she would do the same. . .

'Hi, Katy!'

Joanna rushed up to her side. 'How did the dinner party go last night?'

They walked into the main building of the Rosewall and on to the dining room, Katy describing how well it had gone and how brilliant the Masons were with their planning.

'What about Janine and Mark—they were there too?'

'Yes. Shall we sit by the windows when we've collected our breakfast?'

'Sure.'

From the corner of her eye, Katy saw Mark sharing a table with Bill Lodge. She kept her eyes averted, trying to concentrate upon what Joanna was saying as they sat down amidst the early morning bustle of the meal.

'It had to be quite an interesting evening, I should think,' Joanna was saying. 'A couple of days ago I heard it said that Janine was giving Mark one hell of a rumpus because he didn't get in touch with her during our alert.'

'I don't know about that,' Katy said coolly. 'But last night she did make herself look rather foolish by drinking too much.'

'Wow! I bet that didn't go down very well with the assembled company.'

'Not really. Especially when she announced that Mark was her husband, and that she was preggers.'

Joanna sat back in her chair, aghast. 'You've got to be joking! Did that actually happen, Katy? What on earth did Mark say?'

'Well, nothing much; he just hustled her away from the party as soon as he could.'

'Do you think anybody believed her?'

Katy, to her surprise, was rather impressed at the way

she could recount last evening's happenings so coolly; it was almost as if it had never happened; she felt above it somehow. She shrugged, flicking her long, fair pony-tail back. 'I don't honestly know. I don't care much either.'

'Hey, I thought you were quite taken with Mark?'

'You can go off people, you know,' she laughed casually.

Joanna was looking thoughtful. 'Yes, well, I must say, he's not much of a husband if he's run off and left his wife, and pregnant at that. Now she's caught up with him perhaps he won't be quite so high and mighty as he is at times.'

Katy couldn't repress a sense of loyalty regarding one of her colleagues; the work situation was totally apart from the private. She said quietly, 'On the whole, I haven't found him too bad workwise.'

'Anyhow,' Joanna declared dismissively, 'I think he's a dark horse—probably the sort of man who likes a change of woman with monotonous regularity. . .'

Katy stood up suddenly. 'Sorry, Jo, I must fly; I have rather a lot to do upstairs this morning.'

Joanna was finishing her toast, looking up at her friend quizzically. 'Oh, OK. I didn't think you were too busy up there at present.'

Katy had to escape. For one thing the discussion was becoming too analytical; secondly, she had no wish to collide with Mark Hammond on leaving the dining room.

Once in her office she realised that her casual statement about her workload had not been far from the truth either. They were to expect three admissions for dilatation and curettage, and two women in the first stages of labour would be arriving at any time. But, to be honest, her self-satisfaction at how she was handling Joanna's questions had quickly run out of steam. She could not talk about Mark a moment longer.

As it transpired, Katy was not required to. Miss Munro told her that Mr Hammond was leaving directly after breakfast and would be away for a few days in London. He had been asked to give an important lecture at the Royal College of Obstetricians and Gynaecologists, and would also be visiting the baby unit at the Hospital for Sick Children, in Great Ormond Street.

Later in the week, Katy was glad of a respite to spend three days with her family at Clacton. Katy had an idea it was Miss Munro's way of thanking those who'd worked well during the floods on a rota basis.

At her mother's home, Katy relaxed, and, more than anything, seeing Fleur's brave optimism and the love she and her brother had for each other helped Katy get a grip on her own affairs.

Strangely, her mother seemed to sense that things were not too happy for Katy, and on their last afternoon together, while walking along the water's edge, having the broad beaches to themselves after the holiday-makers' exodus, they talked in a way that had not been possible during the shock period after Steve had revealed himself for what he really was, having let her whole family down, in a sense. Now her mother gave her a searching look.

'You know, Katy, you'll find someone else, I'm sure of it— or love will find you. All that you've been through and the way you have dealt with it has made you strong and more able to handle these relationships that go awry. I don't know, but you might have already met someone else since at Rosewall, and even that may not have turned out to be perfect; nevertheless, these things are all steps towards an ultimate happiness that will emerge for you, I am absolutely sure.'

'Thanks, Mum, it's lovely talking to you this way. . .'

'I'll tell you something, Katy. Whatever happens in

the future, if you find yourself falling in love again, even if it doesn't lead to the real thing, and if you feel like it, darling, come down here to talk it over. Don't think I'm such an old fuddy-duddy that I don't understand! I've learned a lot too, you know, since the business with Steve.

'So—' her mother took her arm lovingly '—just you take life as it comes and enjoy yourself, but the main thing is not to think that your world has come to an end if a normal, straightforward love affair just does not work out. . .'

In the train going back to Maldon, Katy went over her mother's well-meaning words. It was a very comforting feeling that they could at last talk openly now since the troubles that had shaken their family to the core, especially in the wake of her father's death.

But Katy had not had a 'straightforward love affair', by which her mother meant with a man who was free and unmarried. And what would be her mother's advice upon that?

By the time she'd returned to Rosewall and was back in her welcoming little flat, Katy knew the answer only too well. But could she forget him? Could she put the rapport that had been so obvious between them both from her as if it had never happened? Would she be able to further disregard Mark's pleas for her to listen to his explanation?

It was not until she was inside the flat that Katy noticed the envelope on the mat. It was addressed to her, and she knew without doubt that it was from Mark. Her first instinct was to tear it into tiny pieces, but instead she left it on the coffee-table, switched on the fire, put on the kettle, showered and changed into trousers and sweater. Then, once curled up on the settee with her coffee, she slit open the envelope, hands trembling, the large, bold handwriting making her heart thud as she began to read.

Dear Katy,

I fully understand your reaction, but I must see you; I cannot carry on like this. At least allow me a hearing. If you do and afterwards are still of the same mind, that must be for you to decide. I tried to see you when I returned yesterday but was told you had gone home. Perhaps you would leave an answer to this note in my downstairs office when you are back.

Mark.

Katy read the letter over and over again. Sometimes it made sense in the tumult of her thoughts, sometimes it didn't.

In bed that night, the only thing she did know was that she would talk to him, but simply in order to keep their working relationship on a businesslike footing. In the morning, she rose early to write a short, curt note to Mark that gave little or nothing away as to the true devastation of her feelings. All of that had to be forgotten as if it had never happened. It was with great trepidation she got ready to go on duty, wondering how she would feel on coming face to face with Mark for the first time since the dinner party.

Once downstairs, she left the note on his desk, then went into breakfast. Luckily she sat alone, which was a great relief. Neither was there any sign of Mark, and unhappily now she concluded that the torture would be drawn out until he did the round that morning between ten and eleven.

But her worries were groundless. At ten-thirty Bill Lodge came in with one of the young housemen. 'Morning, Sister!' he greeted her cheerily. 'We haven't too many worries this morning, I think?'

'No.' She smiled. 'This is a trouble-free zone, Doctor!'

'I'm relieved to hear it. The young woman having a hysterectomy today has had a good night, then?'

'Yes, apparently. She seems quite bright.'

'And what about the eighteen-year-old?'

'Well, she was nervous when she was admitted yesterday, but seems less troubled now,' Katy told him.

'She's the girl with the menstrual disorder, isn't she? She's down on my theatre list for a D and C, so that will not be until four o'clock this afternoon; the other two will follow, and that's the end of my list.'

They completed the round and Bill Lodge finished his notes in the office. He tucked his pen into the top pocket of his white coat with rather more emphasis than Katy thought necessary as he said hesitantly, 'Katy, I hope you won't mind me asking, but you know Mark pretty well, I believe?'

She took a deep breath, and said steadily, 'Well, yes, we work closely together. In fact I was surprised he didn't come in with you this morning.'

'Yes, indeed, although perhaps it's just as well he didn't. He's like a bear with a sore head. One of his patients in the private sector has made a complaint of some sort to Miss Munro. I'm not quite clear what it's all about, but it's sufficient to make Mark well nigh unapproachable. . .'

He glanced up at the ceiling and around the room, his benign-looking features troubled as his eyes returned to her. 'Quite honestly I think there's much more than that bothering him. I heard about this business at the party; I don't know how true any of it is, and I wasn't able to be there myself. Nevertheless, something's upsetting him badly and—well, as we work together and usually get on fine, I just felt I had to ask if you might be able to throw any light on it. I mean, very often a woman spots these things.'

'Well. . .I was at the party, Bill, and all I know is that his woman friend, Janine, has now announced the fact that they are married and she is pregnant. Rather indiscreetly she chose the night of the party to tell everybody. As you can imagine, Mark was not too pleased, but there's little more I can say, I'm afraid. They left after the commotion it caused.'

Bill Lodge sighed. 'Yes, that's much the same as I heard. He's been a bit of a fool by the look of it. . .'

Katy finished her shift by nine that evening and decided to have an early night and cook something in her mini-kitchen. She had just finished when the phone rang, and it was Mark, his voice flat and distant.

'Mark here, Katy. I have your note. Can we meet in my office in about half an hour?'

'If you wish, but, Mark, it must be brief. I have other things to do,' she said, sounding not in the least as she felt.

Later on her way downstairs she tried to do a run-through of what she would say but found it impossible. While tapping on his door she would have given anything to rush away.

He wasn't seated at his desk. He wore much the same as she did—sweater and jeans. Only the grim set of his face was different, and the dejected slump of his shoulders before he stood up and pulled a chair forward for her. He remained standing then, just leaning against the desk. Their eyes met briefly. His dark hair was ruffled slightly, a faint stubble of shadow masked the strong square jaw, and his slim hands were thrust into his jeans pockets as he glanced down now at the carpet, then back at her, saying quietly, 'Katy, I cannot apologise enough for the other night. Janine was. . .'

Just being alone with Mark was making her go to pieces. She interrupted him with a wave of her hand. 'I haven't come down here to discuss Janine, Mark, but merely, as I said in the note, to establish that we'll be able to work together in some kind of. . .harmony. If not, I'll apply for a transfer to another department. It shouldn't be too difficult.'

'I think you're rather leaping ahead, Katy. All I want

to do is explain fully why Janine acted as she did. I have no intention of sweeping this thing under the carpet any longer.'

'I just don't want to know,' she said tersely. 'You have your reasons, I have mine. All I will say is that whatever explanations might be forthcoming from you nothing is going to change my mind. . .'

He stood up suddenly, a light of anger in his eyes as he took a step closer to her. His voice was very controlled, yet it contained a steely note that made him formidable as his jaw tightened and his expression hardened.

'Do you mean to tell me that after all we have said and done together you are not going to allow me to put my case? Even a prisoner in the dock has that opportunity. I thought you had more compassion in you, but I must have been mistaken all along!' The sarcasm in his voice reverberated in her brain.

She was shaking now, realising how great was the feeling running between them. 'You're a fine one to talk about compassion in me!' she burst out in near-hysteria. 'Instead of wasting your time blaming someone else, shouldn't you be at your wife's side, looking after her?' Katy's words rose angrily; her voice trembled as she tried to fight down the tears. 'Perhaps you've already forgotten that she's pregnant!'

She turned from him, her face contorted with anguish and the bitterness of her feelings. Yet she blamed herself now, for this whole thing was in danger of becoming a slanging match because she had lost her temper. . . Blindly she made her way to the door. 'I have to go. . . and besides, this is no place for such a discussion!'

With two strides he was ahead of her at the door, planting himself across it so that there was no way she could get past him. He stared down at her, no words passing his lips, only the cold eyes speaking volumes. She saw despair there, shock, but most of all the almost blunt refusal to accept the way she was treating him—something he had obviously not expected of her.

Yet, in seconds it seemed to render him incapable of further aggression. His broad chest rose and fell as he said with glacial politeness, 'I agree, this certainly is no place for such a discussion. Perhaps tomorrow evening at nine, when I believe we are both off duty, the Blue Boar might be a possibility for dinner, where—' he gave her a hard look '—rational-minded people can sit and talk relatively undisturbed.'

She ignored the barbed hint, feeling her hackles rise again as he moved from the door, allowing her to pass through it.

'I'll be ready at nine tomorrow evening,' she said as she swept past him, still shaking like a leaf, but chin up high.

'Right. I'll pick you up outside the nurses' home.'

And once back in her flat she allowed the tears of misery and love to fall unrestrained.

CHAPTER NINE

THE Blue Boar was a conventional hostelry in the town, which provided comfort and good food, but that evening Katy, as she and Mark dined at a table for two in the half-empty dining room, was already convinced it was the most awful meal she had ever sat down to. For a start she was so wound up that she found it difficult to swallow. When she did manage it, everything tasted the same, and ultimately she gave up.

'I'm so sorry, Mark; I'm afraid I can't possibly tackle this food. I'm really not hungry. . .'

He placed his cutlery together on the plate, pushing it aside slightly, giving her a joyless smile that wrung her heart and saying quietly, 'Nor me, I'm afraid. Don't worry about it. I'll get the waiter to bring us some coffee into the residents' lounge; I'm sure they won't question it now that most of the holiday-makers have left.'

The staff were only too pleased to accommodate them, and once they were settled in high-backed wing-chairs with a small table between them Katy poured the coffee, saying hesitantly, 'I feel this is the least I can do; it isn't that there was anything wrong with the food—'

'Katy, please stop worrying about such trivia when we are here to talk things over, and I really do implore you to listen to what I have to say—'

She interrupted, not wanting him to be under any illusions that she might be persuaded to change her attitude towards his mendacity in keeping the fact from her that he was married.

'Mark, whatever you intend saying, whatever your

explanation, you gave the impression that you were free to do as you chose, that you'd left this woman behind and intended to make a fresh start. To me, that sounded reasonable. I took you at your word as we were friends, especially when you said you wished to confide in me about Janine turning up unexpectedly as she did. . .'

Her voice faltered, then her words petered out. She had vowed she would not make an utter fool of herself, and now it looked as if that was a distinct possibility as she fought back the tears.

Mark's face was immobile as he watched her. He wanted to take her in his arms when she looked so distressed. Was it such a short time ago that they had declared their love for each other and talked of a future together? And now this. Once again Janine had got her own way. He dared not appear to soften towards Katy. She was adamant that he was in the wrong—badly so. And of course, as far as she knew, he was.

The sigh of desperation that he hauled up from the region of his lungs before he answered was almost torture. When eventually he did speak, his voice did little justice to the deep emotion he would have preferred to convey, but he endeavoured to put over the fact that he was not quite the scoundrel she was hinting at.

'Yes, Katy, everything you have said is correct. But I am sure you are beginning to know Janine now as I do. She is weak, selfish and unreliable. I have believed her and trusted her so many times, only for it to reveal itself otherwise. Yes, OK, I misled you over certain things I told you, or didn't tell you, and yet, when Janine put in an appearance, I was desperate for someone to talk to—someone who seemed understanding and level-headed.'

He threw his hands out as if recalling the dilemma he had been in at the time, then went on. 'When I spoke to you and you agreed to have dinner with me, the relief was immense. I looked upon you as a friend and colleague. Also at that time I was under the impression that you had a boyfriend and were happily established; therefore, you seemed well suited to give your opinion without it appearing that I was trying to intrude upon that friendship.'

He gazed at her briefly, the sapphire-blue shirt she wore with a pale silk suit highlighting her eyes to an intensity he had not seen before; their beauty seemed to hold him spellbound. . .until he realised she was speaking.

'I gave you my opinion in good faith, Mark. You do not need me to go over the rest. I'm the one who has made an idiot of myself believing in you. . . It seems to be a bad habit of mine. However, please, may we get this over with?'

By now several people had entered the room; they were no longer able to speak in anything but low whispers, and it gradually dawned upon Mark that he had been the idiot in bringing Katy to this place. Nevertheless, he would tell her the truth and brace himself before seeing the coldness in her eyes and a rejection of everything they had been to each other.

'Katy,' he said quietly, 'I told you how Janine was drunk on the night before I left Brunei. Her behaviour was nothing unusual then, neither had it been so very different for most of the entire time I had known her. I was lonely then, and, to be honest, I quite liked the idea of marriage although I did not say as much to Janine. Nevertheless, as you know, she is able to show two sides of herself, and I suppose I saw the best of her when she wanted something. I—'

'Mark! Katy! Fancy seeing you here! Can we join you?' Joanna burst in, with Ron Green of all people; he was using a walking stick but beaming at them both.

Mark rose from his seat, his polite smile and courteous invitation giving no hint of his frustrated annoyance. 'How nice to see you both,' he said. 'Do sit down.' Katy, already in such a state of misery, hardly cared what was said; as far as her talk with Mark was concerned it seemed to be at an end already.

'I didn't know this was one of your places; do you normally come in here?' Katy smiled as brightly as she could at Joanna.

'She doesn't, Katy; I practically went down on my knees to get her to agree.' Ron grinned happily. 'Now, girls, what are you going to have? And you, sir—a whisky?'

A full hour passed with much talk about the hospital and general work. The evening wore on until the taxi, ordered previously to take them back to Ron's home, as he was still on sick leave, whisked him away with Joanna.

Katy sighed. 'It seems this evening wasn't such a good idea after all.'

Mark said nothing, but called for the bill and settled it while Katy collected her coat from the ladies' room. She was tired and dispirited. The entire evening had been pointless. It was obvious that Mark was about to tell her that he was married to Janine, and, whatever his future plans had been, the pregnancy would alter things completely.

'I want to go straight back to the hospital, please, Mark,' she told him, when they met in the foyer.

On their way out towards the car park, he vaguely noticed a spectacular yellow harvest moon illuminating everything around them. How swiftly life changed; human relationships were so tenuous. Silently he started the BMW and quickly left the town for the country lanes and low hedges; neither of them spoke, but the car was heavy with tension.

Katy could have wept at the way the evening had gone. All she wanted was an arrangement between them that they might still work together amicably; at the same time Mark insisted he tell her the true facts as to how Janine fitted into his life.

As if interpreting her thoughts, Mark suddenly pulled the car off the lane down which they were travelling and brought it to a stop in front of a five-bar gate. Without a word he switched off the engine and turned to her, not touching her; in the moonlight his eyes seemed to burn into hers.

'If we have to stay here all night, Katy, we are going to thrash this thing out!'

'And supposing I don't want to "stay here all night", as you put it? I think you're taking rather a lot for granted, Mark, don't you?' Her words sounded cold and hostile, but beneath that harsh veneer her heart was beating like a drum because just nothing could prevent her wayward body from responding to his at such close proximity. How she hated herself, how she hated him—yet she knew, as soon as the words formed in her mind, that she meant nothing of the sort. Nevertheless, as far as he was concerned she had to make him think it. . .

His voice was as cold as hers now. 'No, Katy, I take nothing in this world for granted, and, incidentally, have I your permission to carry on talking now about the subject uppermost in both our minds?'

She did not move an eyelash at the sound of his voice but doggedly fixed her gaze ahead to where darkened fields lay bathed in shadowy light from the sky. Mist hung suspended above the soil, an odour of decaying grasses emanating from the flood-drenched earth where, so recently, ripened corn had been cut in the heat of the sun. Now, two silent nocturnal bats swooped briefly in their flight, black against the moon. Her reply was a mere whisper. 'Yes, please do. . .' She was not unaware of the slight hint of sarcasm in his voice, but wanted only to retain her waning composure until this encounter was over.

'Very well. If you remember, I was trying to explain

Janine's duplicity in her dealings with me. Her main aim, as I later realised, was to get married. It was something new—something that most of her friends had done and she hadn't. I have never thought for a moment that true love came into it, or perhaps only in my imagination in those initial days when she was trying her hardest to get me to go along with her ideas. Her father, of course, was only too delighted to have a son-in-law. . .'

She turned round to face him in her seat, knowing what was coming next when his eyes locked unflinchingly on hers, his long jaw taut when he saw the stony expression on her face as he continued. 'And only weeks later, when she'd contrived to make the event "the wedding of the year", we were married in Bandar Seri Begawan. . .' His voice had dropped; it was as if the scene he described had temporarily taken over his thoughts. . .until hearing Katy's voice.

'I see, Mark. That's all I need to hear now. Thank you for telling me.'

'Katy, there's more.'

'Mark, there can be nothing more that concerns me.'

'Well, I'm afraid there is more that concerns me!' He felt trapped, hamstrung, caught in a net of his own making, and this woman in front of him—the one who he knew was the love he had searched for all his life—now, judging by the expression on her face, really hated him. 'Katy,' he pleaded, 'you have to listen to my side of things. I want to tell you exactly what I've been doing, such as separating from Janine, getting a new job at Rosewall, making a fresh start. . .'

Katy was shaking her head, thrusting her hands over her ears. 'Mark, I just don't want to hear any of it! It's up to you from now on how you handle your affairs; I want no part of it!' Her voice broke into a hysterical sob. 'Can't you see? Having just extricated myself from one hell in my life, I have no intention of getting embroiled in another!'

Almost automatically he placed his hand upon hers, which she immediately withdrew quickly, as he said in a low, self-deprecating tone, 'I know, Katy. Believe me, when you told me about it my admiration for you knew no bounds at the way you have overcome so much. Even the way you and I became friends—in the beginning—proved that you were prepared to make a fresh start with your own life. Of course I see now how my private affairs must appear to you. . .'

For a brief moment he buried his head in his hands, then looked up at her with the frank gaze she knew so well. 'I had no premeditated ideas of conducting any sort of affair with you, Katy. Janine's arrival was the biggest shock I received, and her behaviour at the Masons' dinner party when she made her announcement was something I shall never, ever forget in my whole life.'

'I see. Well, I only hope that your excellent memory remains with you at least until your child is born,' Katy said caustically.

For one awful moment she thought he was going to round upon her, and she flinched away from him slightly.

With a noisy intake of breath before expelling it, he muttered her name, dragging on every letter. 'K-a-t-y, sarcasm does not become you. This discussion is getting us nowhere!'

He immediately switched on the car engine, as if almost relieved to do something, and backed straight out into the lane in one smooth manoeuvre. Neither spoke on the remaining drive back, and outside the nurses' home he braked but did not cut the engine. Neither did he turn to look at her, only stared straight ahead, saying, 'Just one more thing, Katy: there will be no difference in our relationship at work. Everything will and should be as it was when I first joined the staff. Is that understood?'

He got out of the car and opened the passenger door for her.

'Yes, thank you, Mark. Goodnight.'

She didn't look back as she ran up the steps; it was sufficient to hear the explosive zoom of the car as he shot away into the night, and despite all that had been said that evening the misery of it as Katy went up to her flat was breaking her heart.

In the days following the ill-fated dinner with Mark, Katy did her utmost to go to work each day as if nothing had happened and Mr Hammond, the senior consultant, was a comparatively new member of staff with whom they all got on reasonably well.

At least that was what she told herself, although at times one day seemed as long as a week. She was aware that word had gone around about Janine and of all the speculation it had engendered. And one afternoon when it was fairly quiet on the ward and the weather had settled to a breezy autumn, with unexpected bursts of pale sunshine giving a certain mellowness overall, Katy decided upon what she felt was a positive measure.

It had not taken very much perception to realise that her two special friends, Tessa and Joanna, were mulling over things regarding her and Mark Hammond, and if only for the sake of the smooth running of Fortune Katy felt she had to give them some idea of the facts. And so, having made up her mind to do so before going off duty that evening, she invited Tessa to her flat the following night, having already asked Joanna, who'd accepted, adding that she'd bring a bottle of wine, too.

Tessa was in the staff cloakroom with her. 'Katy, I know there's something worrying you. . .' She looked embarrassed, 'But you don't have to do this, you know. Just because I spilt my troubles into your lap about Roger and me. I mean there's no need. . .'

Katy smiled wanly. 'Tess, I wouldn't do it if I didn't want to. In fact, I'm just longing to talk to someone about everything that's been happening.'

As the lift was full, and there was a group of people waiting, they carried on downstairs, still continuing their conversation. Tessa said, 'I know the feeling, Katy; you can trust me to keep quiet. . .'

'Yes, I'm quite sure of that, Tess. I think Joanna will be the same when she knows the facts rather than other people's guesswork. I—' She broke off suddenly, glancing down at the untidy flight of stone steps in front of them, giving a small wail of exasperation. 'Just look at that litter, Tess; you'd think people would have more consideration, wouldn't you?'

'Trouble is, one can't be sure if it's staff, patients, visitors, or who it is.'

Katy bent down to scoop up the plastic bag that offended her as they reached the turn of the stairs leading to Reception, and at the same time realised there was something else beside old newspapers in it. . . 'Oh, no!'

'What is it?'

'Listen. . .'

Straining their ears, they both heard a thin, pitiful cry. Tessa said quickly, 'Oh, Lord, it sounds like a kitten.'

Katy knelt down and lifted out the newspaper bundle. It contained a newly born baby wrapped in a blood-stained towel. 'No, Tess,' Katy said sadly. 'This is a little girl, and I should say she's just about four hours old.' She handed the child to Tessa, saying, 'Quickly, take her up to Fortune, and I'll ring Mr Hammond immediately from down here.'

Happily Mark was still in the hospital. She called as Tessa ran back upstairs. 'I'll be up on Fortune as soon as I've rung the police!'

* * *

In the intensive care baby unit, the night sister-midwife and Tessa had bathed and weighed the infant, and it was now being warmly wrapped before being fed by catheter. Mark Hammond came in just then with Katy, having met her in the lift, fortuitously with several other people.

'How much does she weigh?' he asked, examining the tiny body.

'Two kilograms,' Tessa told him.

'The cord appears to have been crudely cut. Born in primitive circumstances, I would think. The placenta should have separated. Strange how nature seems to step in and make the third stage take place smoothly. Nevertheless, we must find the mother; she's obviously in need of attention and, at the very worst, infection could develop after several days and kill with septicaemia.

Once the child had been placed in a preheated incubator, Mark Hammond spoke to the police in Miss Munro's office less than half an hour later. And both Tessa and Katy were interviewed regarding how they had discovered the infant.

One of the police constables finished taking his notes, saying with a sad smile, 'We'll do our best to trace the young mother, ma'am; we'll also get in touch with the social services. Meanwhile, sir—' he addressed the consultant '—you'll no doubt keep us informed of any further developments.'

'Of course,' Mark assured them.

Miss Munro thanked them as they left, then said with a sigh to Mark as he made to leave, 'Oh, dear, I do hope the young woman turns up; apart from anything else, if she doesn't, abandoning the baby is going to be quite a serious criminal offence.'

She thanked the two girls for their part in the small drama, and Tessa and Katy, both feeling in sombre mood, went downstairs. Once outside, Katy could see

Roger Maynard's car parked in a discreet corner of the park. Tessa said quickly, 'I expect Roger will wonder where the heck I've been this evening, but thank heaven that little one now stands a chance of life.'

Katy made to take the pathway leading to the nurses' home, saying, 'Let's hope so, Tess. See you tomorrow, then.'

Katy hurried to her flat, knowing only too well how Tess was longing to see Roger, and how the two of them would talk over the events of the day together. She turned the key to her room, wondering how she could bear the lonely hours ahead. It was as if it took the regular rhythm of her working days to reveal exactly the great sense of loss she now felt after the brief joy of Mark's love. However short the affair had been, it seemed that nothing could blot it from her mind.

Mark was in his flat later the same evening. He had poured himself a stiff whisky just as the phone rang. 'Curses,' he muttered under his breath, picking it up. 'Hammond here.'

'It's Janine, Mark.'

Mark took a gulp of his drink before answering, then said as politely as he could, 'Janine, I thought you told me you were going to London this week?'

'I did go away, but not to London,' the voice replied petulantly. 'This call is to tell you that I have no intention of meeting you at the solicitor's office on Friday.'

'What made you change your mind?'

'I haven't changed my mind; it's just that I don't want to talk about ending our marriage when we're about to have a baby together.'

'Look here, Janine! I insist that we do, and that's all there is to it!'

'You insist! My God, you've got a nerve! All you want to do is sleep with that Sister Woods you work with. I have eyes, you know!'

'Janine, I haven't time to waste with you talking such twaddle; if you can't say something worthwhile, don't ring me at all!'

'Look here, sweetie, I'm your wife and don't you forget it! You won't get rid of me that easily, whatever you do. I'm here to stay until the baby's born, after which, by God, I'll make you pay! Don't forget also that there are people at the hospital superior to you, who know that we're married and that you tried to hide it so that you could play the field in your new job. But that job may not last as long as you think when I decide to reveal a few more home truths—'

Mark slammed the phone down. It was utterly impossible to try and talk to that woman without coming up against her threats and lies.

The phone rang again, but he ignored it. Smouldering with anger, he threw on his outdoor gear, unable to remain in the flat a minute longer, and with his mind raging in a fury of bitterness and desperation he went out, his footsteps taking him blindly towards the beach. This seemed to be the only place it was possible to think clearly.

After a night with very little sleep, Katy went on the ward next morning in a state of complete disarray—in mind if not in appearance. She was unable to stop thinking about Mark's short, dismissive end to the evening that she had hoped would be so different from the way it had turned out. She blamed herself for it; the angry retorts and harsh words had only inflamed him. At the outset he had been prepared to put his point, and had she listened to what he had to say that would have been the end of it.

In her dilemma last night she'd found it near-impossible to remain in bed. She had paced the room, and at one stage was so utterly sure she had been in the wrong that she picked up her phone and rang him.

She'd just needed to hear his voice, but without the cutting edge to it that was so unlike him. She'd got the engaged tone. She'd realised then how much she was shaking, and dropped the receiver quickly in something akin to relief, knowing she would not now have to speak to him.

But, still sleepless by one o'clock in the morning, she'd decided she had to walk. She'd dressed and gone out. The moon was up, there was a high wind, and she'd turned her face towards it, needing to go along to the beach in the solitude she loved. Then something warned her against such a rash decision. She thought of her family; should anything happen to her through her own stupidity, she would be to blame for their pain. . .

But, now that she was in the office, thank heaven the tumult in her mind had begun to calm down, especially when, after the night staff had gone, Mark came in to tell her about the abandoned baby. 'Morning, Mark. What's your opinion now that she's taken reasonable feeds and her breathing is improving according to Night Sister?'

He pursed his lips thoughtfully. 'Very good, considering. She's a tough little thing and, although seriously ill, I think she'll pull through.'

'Thank goodness for that. Perhaps we'll hear from the police today about the mother.'

Mark smiled ironically. 'If only. As you know, in cases like this, some young mothers would have rung the hospital to say she was leaving her baby. This one doesn't seem quite so concerned. Also, the child was completely naked, and the birth must have taken place in very primitive circumstances. The woman may need drugs to avoid heavy bleeding too. I believe the police intend putting out messages to this effect. So—' he ran a hand through his dark hair '—that's about all we can do for now.'

'Yes, it's very unsatisfactory. . .' She cast down her eyes to glance through some patients' notes on her desk, while he used the telephone to enquire from Miss Munro if she had heard anything at all about the baby's mother. Katy noticed the dark shadows beneath his eyes, and wondered if his night had been anything like hers. . .

He replaced the receiver, saying wearily, 'No, Miss Munro's heard nothing. Pity I rang,' he said with a wry grin. 'She's just told me we have four pregnant mothers arriving some time today!'

For the rest of the morning, although busy with the new admissions, Katy was always unduly conscious of the fact when Mark did not put in another appearance. Bill Lodge did the rounds, accompanied by the houseman on duty. The four new cases had been admitted and were in various stages of labour, but so far none appeared to be in the nature of an emergency.

Back in the office, Bill was writing up his notes after despatching the houseman to check that all electrical equipment in the labour ward was in good working order now that their portable generators had been serviced following the floods.

'Well, Katy, how are you today?' Bill asked pleasantly. 'I don't seem to have had a chance to speak to you recently.' He smiled, putting his pen away.

'I know, Bill; it's been all go, hasn't it?'

'Still, Mark should be back this afternoon; I understand he has only gone into Maldon on some private business. From what I hear, the poor chap's having a bit of trouble with the woman who turned up out of the blue.' He pursed his lips thoughtfully. 'Damned shame having all this trouble when easing into a new job.'

Katy nodded. 'Well, he certainly has things on his mind at the moment!'

Bill grinned in his usual benign way. 'One thing's for sure, as far as I'm concerned anyway—there are a few compensations in bachelorhood!'

Katy was forced to have a late lunch that day. Sandra was off sick with flu, and one of the part-time auxiliaries could not turn up because her child was running a temperature. Katy had no interest in food these days anyway, and as she toyed with her beef salad she could think only of Mark and the business he was attending to in Maldon. If only she could put his affairs from her mind, but it seemed an impossibility. It would not be an exaggeration to claim that almost every thought she had was in some way connected with him.

'Mind if I join you?' Mark's voice could never be mistaken, and the sound of it made her heart leap with surprise.

'Please do. . .' She smiled; she hadn't thought she would be seeing him quite so soon. If only she wasn't quaking inside, she might be able to dream up something sensible to say. Instead, she passed him the salt and pepper for his lasagne. 'Have you had a good morning?' was the best she could manage.

He gave her an almost tortured smile, his eyes meeting hers briefly as he picked up his cutlery and said, 'Hardly. Nothing is good when it concerns Janine.'

She gave no reply, and for a while they continued their meal in silence, until he remarked flatly, 'As a matter of fact she has taken herself off to London again, no doubt to fritter away some more money.'

Katy pondered on his statement, then tried to be diplomatic. 'Well, I suppose she has quite a lot of time on her hands, Mark, at. . .at present.' Too late she realised that she was referring to the coming baby.

A nerve leapt at Mark's temple. He sighed, two long creases furrowing his brow. 'That's debatable, Katy.' He pushed his plate aside suddenly. 'If you'll excuse me, I have some telephoning to do.'

Katy watched the tall, proud figure stride away, head erect, shoulders back. Already she was beginning to feel infinitely sorry for him, with the extra burden he now seemed to be carrying. She collected a cup of coffee and took it to the small rest room off one of the dining-room alcoves, picking up a magazine, hoping to concentrate her mind upon something else, but it was impossible. The main thought seizing her brain—that Mark had obviously regretted his rash impulse to sit with her and had decided to leave—was like a slap in the face.

That evening both Joanna and Tessa arrived at her door together. They settled themselves down, and Katy poured three glasses of the wine Joanna had brought with her, and, nibbling the cheese straws that Tess had provided, they relaxed into small talk until Katy brought the subject round to Mark Hammond and the current rumours that were spreading. 'I can't help feeling somewhat sorry for him; his work is terrific, and already I've learned a great deal from his modern methods, which, of course, are rather different from the dear old Prof's,' Katy said loyally.

Tessa looked at Katy rather anxiously as Joanna said keenly, 'Yes, I've heard his work is first class. Even so, I suppose he is married to this Janine woman if she says so; she should know, especially if she's pregnant!'

Tessa stepped in as if to protect Katy. 'Myself, I wouldn't think it's much of a marriage from what I've seen. If there is a baby on the way, it's their business, I suppose, but I still think there's something distinctly odd about it all.'

Katy gave her friend a grateful look. 'I think, before we pull anyone else's character to pieces, I'd better tell you girls that before I knew about any of this he and I seemed to have something going for us. I was convinced I was in love with Mark, and he with me. For such a very short time the world had suddenly become a beautiful place, after the way things had been for me before I came to Rosewall.'

Katy gave them a brief résumé of her bigamous marriage, her misery and gradual recovery. She gave a huge sigh. 'I thought he was a free man,' she said pensively. 'But if Mark's going through anything remotely the same as my experience, I can only feel desperately sorry for him.'

Joanna's face was a picture of amazement. 'But Katy. . .why on earth didn't you tell us before? You've always seemed so cheerful, and there was I the other day ribbing you because you didn't blab about your love affairs. God! What you must have gone through! Heaven knows what you thought of me rambling on!'

'Don't give it another thought, Jo.' Katy smiled. 'It was just the way I felt I could handle the situation. Anyhow, that's all in the past now, but with so much gossip going around, which might include my name being linked with Mark's, I felt it time to speak out and at least bring certain things out into the open.'

'I think you're absolutely right, Katy,' Tessa said. 'Now we might be able to help you in some way as we're aware of the facts. You know how things get distorted here. . .'

Joanna was staring into the red glow of the imitation logs, her lustrous eyes romantic, with a far away look in them. 'Funny, isn't it, how so often people are not quite what they seem? I always thought you were so cool, calm and collected, Katy, yet you've had all this stuff going around in your mind, while at the same time doing a super job.' She paused briefly, then sighed. 'But fancy you and Mark Hammond. Oh, it could have been wonderful; you two seem meant for each other.'

Katy shrugged. 'That's just another case of things not being quite what they appear, Jo.'

Tessa gave Katy a conspiratorial smile. 'I can vouch for that. . .' And before Joanna had a chance to ask exactly what she meant she said brightly, 'I'm going out to make the coffee now, Katy; I should think you could do with it.'

'Great, thanks, Tess; everything's ready in the kitchen.'

Joanna was still pondering. 'You know, this rather makes me think more deeply about Ron Green, Katy. I would never have dreamed that the noisy firebrand could be as sentimental as I've discovered. Do you know, the other day he sent me a lovely bunch of red roses. . .'

It was long after midnight by the time the three friends had split up to return to their rooms, Katy having really enjoyed the evening. It was as if unburdening herself of some of the heavier thoughts with which she had been grappling for so long now had her feeling quite light-headed.

She knew she could no longer dream of Mark and herself as a couple, but her past experience and seeing Joanna and Tess so amazed at how she had come through the shock of it all made her wonder again if perhaps she could help Mark do the same by cementing a good basic friendship with him such as they'd had in the early days. Ultimately, he might one day feel as she did at present—that one or two really good friends were worth their weight in gold.

After all, she thought as she became drowsy, that was the most she could ever hope for now.

CHAPTER TEN

NEXT morning, Katy decided she would visit her family at Clacton the next day, Thursday, her day off. The last time she'd telephoned all had been going well. Fleur was recovering, and Ross could soon be coming home to work in London for three months. So it seemed an optimistic time to go.

Katy had been down to collect the post, and was now back in the office, about to prepare the drugs trolley. At the same moment there was a tap on the door, and Melanie rushed in. 'Sister, could you come, please? It's Mrs Chapman; she was brought in yesterday with signs of an early pregnancy. She's complaining of a one-sided lower abdominal pain with vaginal bleeding. She looks awful. . .'

Swiftly Katy pushed the drugs trolley into the cupboard and locked it. 'OK, that sounds like an ectopic pregnancy, which Mr Hammond suspected; I'll ring him immediately. In the meantime, Melanie, stay with Mrs Chapman; there could be faintness and vomiting.'

Mark Hammond arrived, and after examining the woman he told her that a laparoscopy was necessary. 'Now, don't worry, Mrs Chapman; we're going to get you down to the theatre immediately.'

The young woman was in tears and, turning to Katy, said, 'Will you ring my husband, please, Sister, and ask him to come? I feel so. . .so. . .miserable.'

'Yes, of course.'

Mark nodded agreement. 'It's fortunate too that you've had nothing to eat this morning. So I'll see you in about a half an hour. Cheer up, lass; everything will be all right.'

Katy proceeded with all the usual preparations in readiness for the theatre, including taking blood for haemaglobin, taking a full blood-count and cross-matching at least two units of blood.

Melanie whispered to Katy suddenly, 'Sister, what about other things, like pubic hair to be shaved and. . . ?'

Katy shook her head. 'Good girl for thinking of it, Melanie, but there isn't time. This is an emergency op that requires immediate surgery. We've done all that's necessary, consistent with safety,' Katy added quickly. 'Staff's taking Mrs Chapman down to the theatre; the porters are here now. You may go with her and look after the notes, Melanie, and wait in the ante-theatre until the job's over.'

Melanie's eyes brightened. 'Thank you, Sister.'

One hour later the telephone rang on Katy's desk. 'Mark Hammond here, Sister. The laparoscopy revealed a tubal pregnancy and we have removed one Fallopian tube. Mrs Chapman has lost the pregnancy, which is very unfortunate as I believe it was longed for, and, of course, there's a ten per cent chance of a further ectopic pregnancy in the remaining tube. But we won't say too much about that until tomorrow possibly, although I shall be up to see her tonight and discuss it with her husband.'

'It's very sad, but she's a young woman, and maybe she'll be lucky in the future.'

He paused for a moment, then said brusquely, 'You are away early this evening, and having a day off tomorrow?'

'Yes, that's right.'

Katy's breath caught in her throat as she wondered what he was about to say, but it was no more than, 'I hope it's a good one for you.'

Between that conversation, receiving Mrs Chapman back into the ward, as well as Tess and her dividing their attention between the ectopic patient and the two normal births within half an hour of each other, Katy had little time to think of Mark Hammond's gruff comments to her, but they returned to her mind as soon as she was able to get away off duty.

Once in her flat, she took a long, warm bath and relaxed as far as was possible, then spent the rest of the evening telephoning her mother and getting ready for the following day, thereafter attempting to settle down to an early night.

Next morning on the train to Clacton Katy felt quite serene, which was a state with which she was not too familiar. It was still very early; she had caught a commuter train, which meant she arrived at her mother's small but attractive house before eleven.

Both Fleur and her mother greeted her lovingly, and thoughts of Rosewall fled temporarily from her mind while they had a newsy gossip over coffee together. The day passed quickly, and when at last it was time to leave they made arrangements for further meetings, and Fleur seemed optimistic about the future.

'The next time I see you will be when Ross is home, I hope, Katy; then you and Mum must both come and stay with us, and we'll go to a few theatres and dinners out, just spoil ourselves for a change!'

'You bet!' Katy laughed. 'And don't forget the shopping at those super London stores; what do you think, Mum?'

Her mother beamed. 'I can't wait! Now, take care, dear, and don't forget to eat, will you? Another few pounds wouldn't even notice on you!'

The train was even pleasanter on the return journey, having more seating room. The only trouble was it began to rain, and by the time they stopped at Maldon it was streaking down. As she came out of the railway station, the prospect of a taxi looked bleak. Katy stood pondering whether to telephone one of the cab companies or simply wait hopefully. The London train had just drawn in, which meant that her chances would be even slimmer on a night like this.

She went out to the exit, scanning the wet dark road, amidst groups of tired looking businessmen and equally tired wives waiting to take some of them home. As the crowd thinned and people were still buying newspapers and disappearing, she suddenly heard a voice behind her call her name, and immediately thought she had been mistaken for someone else. And yet. . . No, it couldn't be. . . But it was!

'Katy! I thought it was you! What are you doing here?'

She hadn't recognised Mark at first. He was wearing a very expensive-looking dark city overcoat, a matching suit, silk tie, appearing every inch at the very least a stockbroker, or exactly what he was—a highly successful consultant. . .

'Mark! I. . . I've been home to Clacton for the day. Fancy seeing you!'

He looked down at her, his eyes hungrily searching every feature of her face, and she glanced away quickly, remembering far too much. 'Well, well, at least perhaps you'll allow me to offer you a lift back?' he said, in that deeply controlled voice that had the power still to make her shake inside.

'I was just waiting for a taxi actually.'

'Had you ordered it, then?'

'No, I was just about to.'

He took her arm gently. 'That's totally unnecessary. Come along, my car's over here.'

He helped her into the BMW, and she sank gratefully into the luxurious upholstery as they set off.

Their conversation was somewhat stilted until Mark suggested suddenly, 'Look, there's a little inn just along here, Katy; you must need a cup of coffee, and I certainly do. What do you think?'

It was automatic for her to say yes. Just to be in his company with no one else around. She knew she was far too soft-hearted, but had a feeling that there was something in particular he had to say to her, and this had given him just the opportunity away from the hospital. 'Why not?' she said as coolly as possible.

They sat on high-backed oak settles, one on either side of a sturdy oak table, the beamed ceiling hung about with all the hunting equipage of two hundred years ago. Mark ordered coffee and the smoked salmon sandwiches offered on the menu. When their tray was brought to them, it carried freshly brewed coffee, and delicious home-made bread, with wafer-thin slices of salmon.

He smiled as she poured the coffee and he set out the plates of food. 'I should think this is quite a place to come to at any time. I've seen it once or twice, but well. . .lately, there's been little time for such pleasures.'

Katy could think of nothing more to say but 'How's Janine?'

Mark gave one of his kindly, gentle smiles, as if appreciating her question. 'Well,' he sighed slowly, 'as a matter of fact I have been to the law courts to see an old friend of mine—a barrister who has rooms there. I had to tell him the whole sorry story, finishing with how Janine insists I am the father of her child.' He frowned slightly. 'Jonathan knew as well as you and I that there can be no positive proof of paternity until a blood test has been carried out; that's the next thing I must insist upon.

'We talked over the pros and cons of leaving her, divorcing, confirming who the child belongs to, and getting Janine out of my life, which, of course, is why I came over here in the first place—to make a fresh start.'

'So really,' Katy said, 'there's very little your friend can advise at this stage?'

'Well, I wouldn't say that exactly. We shall keep in

touch,' Mark said, staring into space.

'I suppose nothing would be gained if you moved elsewhere? Do you think she'd follow?'

'I do, if only for the money.'

They talked on for a while, neither able to come up with any ready solutions. He looked at her suddenly. 'Katy, I want to say so many things to you—' He broke off, then went on quickly, 'How did you find your family?' The remark made it sound as if he had strayed into forbidden territory, then swiftly covered up with a more mundane question.

'Everything seems fine at present, thanks, Mark; my sister-in-law, Fleur, is progressing very satisfactorily.'

'That's splendid. Strange, isn't it, how by simply going away for a day out of one's normal routine it seems to have the effect of creating a quite strong need to catch up with things once back home?'

'Yes. In the train this evening I found myself wondering what had been happening on Fortune, and with everything that revolves around it.'

'Incidentally, so far we've heard nothing about the tiny bag-baby you found, then?'

Katy shook her head. 'Not as far as I know. The mother has not come forward. The police are even less hopeful, I believe.'

'What a tragedy...'

They were silent for a few moments, each with their own thoughts, until Mark said, leaning slightly across the table, 'Katy, I can't tell you how much I've appreciated having a normal conversation with you like this. I think at first that aspect upset me as much as anything—that the deep friendship we'd had was slipping away.'

'No, Mark, I couldn't keep it up. I realise how much worse your problems are now than when I first met you. And well, everyone needs a friend, and I concluded that the fact that I've been... Well, it doesn't matter about that, but I hoped, as I said at the beginning of all this trouble, that we could work together and even eventually become friends again, and maybe this is happening sooner than I thought it would.'

When Mark had paid the bill and they went out to the car, there did not seem an awful lot more to say. Katy didn't feel it was right to indulge in idle chatter when Mark obviously had so much personal trouble on his mind, let alone the strains of his work as well.

They drew to a stop outside her door. 'Thank you, Mark, for tonight. I'm quite glad now that I didn't ring for a taxi,' she said with a smile.

'I certainly am.' He smiled back, and said suddenly, 'If things should get even more difficult with Janine, can we talk again? As I see it, she and I are some way from solving this problem. She's gallivanting off even now with a male friend. I believe it's someone who lives in Surrey; she's obviously forgotten she told me about him when we were in Brunei. He came out to stay for a month, as far as I recall. As you know, she was always trying desperately hard to make me jealous.' His eyes were cold as he spoke, then softened. 'But I mustn't keep you, Katy. See you tomorrow, then. Goodnight. . .'

Katy settled down to sleep much better than she had for days. She just could not generate hate in her heart for someone whom she loved so deeply despite what had happened and the hopelessness of it. Surely the healing that had to take place would be far better than a malignant torture that gradually consumed her? Perhaps one day the scars of loving Mark would fade and die away.

On Fortune next morning, Katy was soon able to catch up on things that had happened while she had been on her day off. Mrs Chapman had come to terms with the trauma of her laparoscopy and after a night of observations made at one hourly intervals was now making satisfactory progress. Katy went to see the young woman, who, although rather tearful, was accepting the new situation bravely.

'It's only just getting through to me, Sister, that I'm no longer pregnant. Tony will be so disappointed,' she said, dabbing her tears.

'My dear, you just get yourself relaxed and well again; I'm sure when your husband comes in he will say exactly the same— Oh, my goodness, what's this?'

A messenger suddenly arrived, carrying a large bouquet of roses for Mrs Chapman. . .who promptly burst into tears again.

'There you are, you see!' Katy beamed. 'This is what he thinks of you. My, they're beautiful!' Katy exclaimed, hearing the telephone ring. 'Do you know, you look as pretty as a picture now? Excuse me just a moment, dear.'

Typical. The wretched thing stopped ringing just as she got there. She went back to close the ward doors carefully, knowing that another highly emotional event was taking place that morning that Mrs Chapman certainly didn't want to see. Two of their very special incubator babies, now having reached an acceptable weight of 2.5 kilograms would be going home with their mothers at last.

All the staff, including the auxiliaries, and even the library lady and wardmaids, were crying when the small gathering of family groups tearfully gave their thanks and farewells.

'Oh, dear,' Katy said shakily, 'let me just have one more look at our babies. And just make sure you all come back to see us again!'

Eventually the cars were waved away, and a cup of tea was provided by a new student nurse just starting her first year of training.

'Thanks, Nurse. Good thinking!' Katy said with approval.

The eighteen-year-old beamed happily. 'I'll never forget those dear, darling babies on my first day, Sister,' she said, her eyes welling up again. 'They were just like lovely little dolls!'

The party had to break up rather hurriedly then, when Mark Hammond arrived to see Mrs Chapman. Everyone dispersed to their appointed tasks, and Tessa brought out the dressings trolley to take to the patient's bedside and closed the curtains. Mark smiled. 'Hello, Mrs Chapman, how are you feeling?'

'OK, thanks, Doctor.'

Mark examined the wound which Katy had uncovered for him. 'Fine,' he announced. 'The wound is a good incision, Mrs Chapman; that has the advantage of being safe and achieves a more acceptable cosmetic result, and as you have no wound drains there should be no haematoma formation.' He went on to explain that he would prescribe an analgesic for her, if and when she needed it, assess the post-operative progress, and any further medical treatment necessary. 'Now, are there any questions?'

'Yes, Doctor. I want to know when we can have sexual intercourse again,' she said softly.

'Well, you should be able to resume in about four weeks. But I must emphasise, Mrs Chapman, that you should only try to conceive when you yourself feel mentally and physically ready to embark upon a pregnancy.' The phone rang and no one appeared to hear it.

'Will you excuse me, Mr Hammond?' Katy said impatiently, when the instrument persisted.

'Yes, of course, Sister; I'll see you in the office.'

Just as Katy arrived at the corridor phone, Tessa appeared, apologising and muttering quickly, 'Sorry, two of the staff are in the airing cupboard with the door closed, the others are in the baby unit. . .'

'It's OK,' Katy said. 'Hello, yes, Sister Woods speaking.'

'It's Joanna Bennett, Katy.' She sounded breathless and quite unlike her usual self. 'We've just had an ambulance admittance down here in Casualty, and I'm sure it's Janine! Could you come down quickly? We can't tell Mr Hammond; it may not be her!'

'OK. I'll be right there!'

Katy's heart was beating furiously as she caught sight of Tessa going into the ward to accompany Mark to the baby unit. 'Tess, I simply have to go downstairs; I won't be long!'

'Something wrong, Katy? You look worried.'

'No, no, it's OK; I'll tell you when I come back.'

In Accident and Emergency, Joanna immediately took Katy to an end cubicle where the curtains were closely drawn. A girl lay unconscious on the bed, bloodied bandages on both wrists. The casualty officer had arrived at the same time and was already dealing with the situation.

Joanna said quickly to Katy, 'They've brought her in from the Golden Fleece Hotel; that's where Janine was, isn't it?' Katy nodded as Joanna went on, 'One of the staff happened to go into her room to change the towels; the bathroom door was open and she was lying slumped over the basin, blood everywhere. It looks as if she's slashed her wrists; difficult to tell yet, but I don't think it's the main arterial vein— a bit too high up for that. . .'

The CO glanced at her. 'You think you know her, do you, Sister?'

Katy nodded, staring at the pale, clammy face, the dark abundance of hair, the closed eyes, and tall, graceful figure beneath the covers, and said swiftly, 'I'm pretty certain it's Janine Hammond; Mark was on Fortune when I came down just now.'

'Well,' the medic said, 'there's no doubt she's had a go at finishing herself off, but not very successfully at that. Nothing to worry about, anyway.'

Katy thanked him. 'I'd better go up and tell Mark, I suppose. The people at the hotel know, but you were right, Joanna, to confirm who it was first. Thanks very much. . .'

Upstairs, as it happened, Katy met Mark coming down. He gave her a surprised smile. 'You dashed off; I wasn't too sure if you were coming back, but I've left the prescriptions with Staff. . .' He looked at her closely. 'Katy, are you all right? What's wrong?'

Katy clenched her hands at her sides, saying as calmly as she could, 'Mark, I'm sorry. . . It's. . .well, it's Janine. She's tried to commit suicide; they've just brought her in. She's OK, lost quite a bit of blood, but they're seeing to her now.'

'My God,' he muttered harshly. 'Are there no lengths to which she'll not go. . .?'

'I'll get back to Fortune, then, if there's nothing I can do,' Katy said, her heart crying out in sympathy with him.

He ran a distracted hand across his face. 'No, Katy. Thank you for telling me; I'll get down there straight away.'

Later that evening, Mark rang just as Katy was drifting off to sleep. 'Katy, it's Mark. Sorry if I woke you.'

'No, it's OK, really. How's Janine?'

'Sound asleep. She hasn't said very much; she's just a child, you know, Katy, at times, despite the malice in her that so often rises to the surface. I just can't help feeling sorry for her. It's as if nothing she tries will satisfy her or make her happy. People like that so often seem to lurch from one disaster to another.'

'Yes, I know what you mean, but unfortunately other people become entangled, and the unhappiness spreads.'

'You're so right. I'll let you get some sleep now. Oh, just one more thing, Katy—I know this sounds callous, but if it happens that one day my troubles with Janine come to an end, would there be any chance at all for us?'

'Mark, that question is like asking how many pebbles there'll be on the beach this time next year. It's impossible to answer. . .'

'I'm sorry, yes, of course. Just forget I ever mentioned it. Goodnight now.'

She couldn't sleep for a long while after his call. She had, perhaps, given the sort of answer he least expected. But how was it possible for her to say yes or no to his question? How long was it likely to be before Janine had long since faded from his life? And, of course, there was the baby. Could it be his. . . ? She was racked with misery and uncertainty, and at last fell into a troubled sleep.

The following afternoon, Joanna told Katy that Janine was staying on the general ward for just one more night and then she would be free to leave. Katy knew she was almost compelled to see how she was and, although it was with some trepidation, when she was due to go off duty that evening she went downstairs to join the few visitors who were just beginning to filter in.

Janine was sitting up in bed reading when Katy approached her. She gave her a nervous smile and put her book aside. 'Hi, Katy. . .' She looked embarrassed, and said, 'I've been a bit of a fool, I suppose you think?'

Katy pulled up a chair with a smile and sat down at the bedside. 'Well, I reckon there are a few easier ways to sort yourself out!'

'Mark's been in and said as much. He said he's coming in again later this evening. There's no need for him to.' She seemed to drift away into her thoughts, her face as white as the bandages on her wrists. Suddenly she said, 'Mark doesn't love me any more, you know. . .'

Katy was still pondering upon her reply to such a remark, when one of the staff arrived, saying with a smile, 'Mr Hammond's just come in. I'll draw the curtains so there'll be a little more privacy.'

Katy stood up. 'I must go, Janine.'

Mark was already at the bedside, drawing the curtains behind him and acknowledging Katy. 'Janine. How are you tonight?'

'I'm OK, thanks,' came the almost sullen reply.

Katy again made to leave, but Mark said quickly, 'Katy, I'll come back later; Janine would prefer your company to mine, I'm sure.'

'Well, at least Katy can tell me how the people are whom we met at the party,' Janine said petulantly, 'but that will have to wait anyhow.' She gave Mark a searching look. 'What about what you asked me this morning about having a blood test carried out here at Rosewall instead of Harley Street, to prove the paternity of the baby?'

'Yes, I've already arranged for Bill Lodge to deal with it. He'll be here about nine this evening.' Mark's face was tense. 'I'm certainly not altering that, whatever you say!'

'And I am telling you now that I am not going to have it done!' Janine's features were suddenly suffused with high colour in her determination. 'I am not pregnant!' she shouted.

Mark exploded. 'Janine! What are you saying, for God's sake? You don't mean the whole thing from when you announced it at the party has been one gigantic lie from start to finish?'

Katy's heart was thumping. Could Janine possibly mean what she was saying. . . ?

The girl gave Mark a smug smile. 'That's exactly what I do mean!' She sank back on her pillows as if finding the effect of her words utterly amusing.

Mark's voice was almost inaudible as he muttered, 'And then you tried suicide! I see! You scheming little. . .'

Katy stood up quickly, grasping Mark's arm. 'Mark, shouldn't you leave this discussion until you are somewhere in private?'

Mark's voice shook her hold from him. 'No. Perhaps it wouldn't be a bad idea to get it all over with in public!' He heard the ward doors being closed, even though the few patients there were in the TV room. 'You purposely planned all of this so that it occurred before the decree absolute came through, didn't you? Well, as it happens, I received mine this very morning, after agonising days of waiting, I can tell you! And you will no doubt find yours when you return to your hotel. . .I just cannot believe you could be so despicable!'

He had risen slowly from his chair, glowering at her. 'How dare you? How dare you go to such lengths to pretend I still mean something to you, when, in actual fact, our divorce was based on your adultery over a year ago! All you wanted was to stir up trouble and try to resume your disgraceful way of life, and I was paying for it!

'Why do you think I was in touch with the best legal brains between here and Brunei? I simply wanted to get on with my life and my job! That was all I intended when I arrived in England. But you couldn't bear to see me trying to make a fresh start, could you? Think of the people here whom you've upset all because of your callous selfishness and greed!'

Janine was looking less sure of herself by now. 'How do I know you're not lying to me about the completion of the divorce?'

'Because, Janine—' he suddenly dropped his voice as if all the fight had gone from him and he no longer had the inclination or the need to argue with her '—your life is your own again now. Whatever you do is your decision. . .whether you lie or not. I do not lie. . . Just remember that.'

Tears of self-pity suddenly appeared in her eyes. 'Anyway, I have already ordered my plane ticket back to Brunei for next week, Mark. My friend from Surrey is coming out there too, he's asked me to marry him once I am free.' She looked down at her wrists and dashed her tears away. 'I haven't yet made up my mind. I might even take up my physiotherapy work again. . .'

Katy had to leave. Neither Mark nor Janine noticed.

Once back in her rooms, Katy could only sit and go over everything she had heard, experiencing a tumult of sympathy for Janine's unstable behaviour, regrets—the wasted time and love that Katy herself had gone through—as well as heartache for Mark. And now she was simply left in a wilderness. It was difficult not to feel an element of self-pity.

Two days following the tirade between Mark and Janine, Miss Munro, who had been told the details, confided to Katy that Mr Hammond was taking a fortnight off to finalise things, both legally as well as financially, before Janine flew back to the other side of the world. The SNO had called her to her office, and they were at present sitting over tea together.

'A charming man, Katy, but some men can never spot a scheming woman, unfortunately.' She looked at the young sister in front of her. 'You have been through a great deal, my dear, and overcome it; let's hope he can do the same. I did hear that he had been asked to do some more lecturing in the near future, but we shall see.'

Work had always been the best possible thing for anyone with problems on their mind, Katy thought, and she was no exception. Bill Lodge had been standing in for Mark since he'd gone away, and a new young registrar was on the staff until the senior consultant returned.

Bill was chatting away to Katy in the office a week

later. It was a bright and sunny morning, even though November was already with them. 'Well, I'd better be on my way, Katy. I hope to see you at our pre-Christmas dance in two weeks' time.'

'Well, I'll think about it, Bill; no one's asked me to go yet, though!'

'Early days yet, Woodsy,' he laughed; he used Katy's nickname when he felt somewhat skittish, which was not too often.

She sighed when the door closed. Just lately she had felt extremely dejected. After all the business with Mark and Janine she had somehow expected to receive a phone call or note from Mark. But apparently, instead of returning to Rosewall, he had indeed, as Miss Munro had indicated, taken on a series of lectures over various parts of the country, and no one seemed to know when he intended returning to Rosewall.

She couldn't really blame him if he didn't come back at all. There had been so much unhappiness from the time of his arrival. Yet there had been happiness too, as she reminded herself so often, but that was almost a dream now, one that faded more as each day passed, and at times she wondered if it had ever happened at all. Maybe that's all it really was—she had fallen in love with a dream of her own making. . .

The following week everyone was beginning to talk about the forthcoming dance. Tessa was going with Roger, whose wife sadly was now confined to an iron lung in a nursing home, Joanna was going with Ron Green, who seemed to be a changed man since Joanna had become interested in him, and even young Melanie and Sandra were talking about the boyfriends they were bringing.

All this stirred up the old familiar pangs of loneliness in Katy, and by the time the night of the dance arrived, although she had told friends she would be going, in her heart Katy decided it was impossible. Mark still haunted her, and until her mind was free of him those social occasions were more of a burden than a pleasure.

She had promised both Tess and Joanna that she would see them at the dance but had not been sure what time she would be there. In order to feel that she was not being entirely dishonest with her two friends, Katy dressed with care that evening in her black dress. She wished she possessed another in a way, when she remembered the compliments she had received from Mark the first time she'd worn it. Nevertheless, it was the only decent one she possessed, and she carried on putting finishing touches to her hair, and brushed its gleaming tresses to her shoulders.

She slipped into black patent, medium-heeled courts. This familiar activity made her feel better and, finally adding some of her favourite perfume, she collected her coat and bag and went downstairs.

With rising spirits, she decided to go across to the large gymnasium where their dances were usually held, telling herself that she would just look in. Music was already drifting through the window. Holly and mistletoe and silver and gold Christmas decorations graced walls and ceiling. As she neared the large double doors thrown open to the unseasonably mild night, a couple came out arm in arm, the girl laughing up into the face of one of the junior housemen who occasionally worked on Fortune.

Suddenly, Katy felt unable to go any further. She turned around abruptly to retrace her steps. Yet, still fascinated by the beauty of the night, once reaching the nurses' home, she carried on walking through the little wicket-gate, passed the silent marina and on to the beach, where the river, now devoid of holiday craft, unfurled itself in long, shallow waves over the pebbles.

Katy paused briefly, looking out beyond the estuary. In the far distance a lighted ship slid silently along the ruler-straight horizon—bound for where? she wondered. There was the rest of the world out there. Was it time for her to move on again, find another job in some far distant land. . . ?

Pensively she walked on, her thoughts as ever returning to Mark, and what might have been. Now that he was free of Janine, maybe he too intended leaving Rosewall. . .

Her feet scrunched over the sandy pebbles; she stood for a moment listening to the water as it met the shore. About to walk on, she imagined she heard the sound of footsteps on the shingle behind her, but then decided it was nothing. But a few minutes later she was sure she heard other footsteps apart from her own.

She half turned as she walked, but all she could see was the old skeleton wreck of a fishing boat left to the vagaries of the weather. Nevertheless, she realised that she had perhaps walked further than she'd intended. It was far more desolate and wild where the river rushed to the open sea, and a strong breeze stirred her hair about her face.

A sudden fear seized her, and, feeling unsure of herself, she realised how foolish she had been to come to such a place now that summer had gone. Quickening her steps, she neared the old wooden hull, giving it a wide berth as she hurried by. Then a dark figure stepped from the shadows, and, giving a terrified gasp of fear, Katy began to run for all she was worth, but her unsuitable shoes slowed her down badly. Until a man's voice called, 'Excuse me. . .'

She made a gigantic effort to sprint forward, but it was no use; the footsteps gained on her, and she felt a touch on her arm, heard herself scream out, then the man's voice shouted, 'Katy! Katy! It's all right, it's Mark!'

By now, nearly fainting with shock, she turned, and It was him! His dark overcoat was unbuttoned, his hair ruffled, as he gasped, 'Oh, my God, Katy, it is you! I can't believe it!' Automatically his arms had reached out to her, and they were holding each other as if for support in the shock of the moment, Mark staring down into her face as if she had just risen from the waves. 'Oh, my dear, I was hoping to see you, certainly not here, but at the dance!'

At last Katy was able to speak, and pushed her hair back from her lovely face, her eyes larger and more brilliant than the stars above as Mark feasted his eyes upon every beloved feature. 'Mark, wh-where have you come from?' she stammered breathlessly. 'It's so amazing. . .I just didn't want to go into the dance, and decided to come up here before. . .well. . .going to bed, actually!' she said with a little grin.

Mark couldn't take his arms from her, and said, 'Well, I'd previously talked to Bill Lodge on the phone this morning, and he said he thought it pretty certain you were coming to the dance as he'd overheard you chatting to friends about it. So I was determined to find you! But as you did not seem to be anywhere around in the dance hall I asked one of our young housemen if he'd seen you. He said he thought it could have been you he saw returning to the nurses' home. . .'

Katy gave a tinkling laugh of sheer joy. Quite suddenly everything had been turned on its head. Just to be at Mark's side again made her incapable of normal thinking. 'Um. . .yes, that's right, I did see him, then decided to take a walk. . .just to think really.'

'Exactly what I'd hoped! Then, of course, when I saw that lonely figure on the beach just now, I didn't quite know how to approach the person in case it wasn't you. . . Oh, Katy, my dear, how are you? It seems so long. So much has happened. . .'

Quite suddenly, they both stood absolutely still. Moonlight and shadow lapped around them and the stars looked down from above. Mark's arms slowly enfolded her; he held her to him, and gradually, very gradually, their eyes meeting, Mark's lips brushed hers tenderly. 'Katy,' he whispered. 'Katy, darling, there is so much I want to say. . .' They clasped each other's hands as if melded together. . .

'Mark,' she said tremulously, heart racing with anxiety and joy, 'are you back here for good, or is it just for the dance?'

'To hell with the dance, my love. I told Bill I was coming back to claim you if you'll have me; he knows what it's all about, and had I not found you this evening I'd have gone on searching wherever you were. . .'

Katy sighed blissfully, but tried to apply a little common sense to her mental powers; with Mark in such close proximity it was almost impossible. 'Mark, just tell me, why did you never mention you were so close to getting your divorce through when you first talked about your problems with Janine?'

'Because, my darling, I didn't want you to think I was trying to lure you from that boyfriend—who, of course, I didn't know at the time was fictional! Neither did I want you to think I had any designs upon you. Now it seems we were both being cautious for the very same reason.'

'And Janine? Has she gone back to Brunei now? Is everything completely over between you?'

'Absolutely over, Katy. Janine received her divorce papers, as I said she would.' He drew her into his arms, their hearts beating as one. Their lips met and sealed the love they knew had never left them.

Several minutes later, arms clasped about each other, they walked slowly back to where the bright lights of the hospital beckoned. The strains of a love song floated out to them on the velvety silence of the night. Mark held her to him again.

'Sweetheart, our problems are over now. We shall no longer be troubled with Janine; that part of my life is over and done with. Ours is only just beginning. You know how much I love you—always have and always will. I'm sure it was love at first sight for me.'

'Me too, Mark. I'm utterly convinced of it.' They reached his car where it stood on the nurses' home drive. Briefly they lingered there as Mark caressed her face tenderly. 'Katy, I was so unsure of my reception when I eventually caught up with you tonight, but I must ask you, my darling, is marriage something you never wish to risk again?'

'Mark, doesn't the same question apply to you also?'

He nodded. 'I have to say, sweetheart, that whether we go for marriage or just living together our love is the main thing. I am right, aren't I, Katy? Tell me I'm not presuming anything. I need you with me for the rest of my life, and have to know that you feel exactly the same.'

'My darling,' she whispered, caressing his cheek with her hand. 'You should know that by now. I am nothing without you, and we have all the time in the world to work things out together.'

'In that case,' he laughed happily, 'we shall have a pre-honeymoon, then maybe one day a wedding to which all our friends and family will come; that will be an excuse for another honeymoon!' He chuckled.

Her eyes shone. 'Mark, remember the floodtide, our going out on the boat and everything? Well, I think we're going to be involved in another, where everything happens at once. But oh, heavens, what an occasion it's going to be!'

Five minutes later, dancing with Katy in his arms, seeing no one else but the future love of a lifetime, Mark whispered, 'You look divine in that dress, Katy. This is our world just beginning. . .'

And to Katy, Rosewall—and everyone in it—seemed to be the most wonderful place in the world.

MILLS & BOON®

Medical Romance™

COMING NEXT MONTH

A GIFT FOR HEALING by Lilian Darcy

Camberton Hospital

Karen Graham's manipulative ex-boyfriend, who was sick with TB, wanted her back. Guilt-ridden, she had no-one to turn to except Lee Shadwell. He was more than willing to offer friendship and support. Karen knew she was loved and in love, but with which man?

POWERS OF PERSUASION by Laura MacDonald

Nadine vowed to remain immune to the charms of the new Italian registrar Dr Angelo Fabrielli. But that proved impossible when he moved into her house—and her heart! But she refused to be his wife knowing that she could never give him the one thing he needed most...

FAMILY TIES by Joanna Neil

The new locum, Dr Matthew Kingston, was critical and a touch too arrogant so Becky Laurens kept her distance. But that proved difficult when she found him incredibly attractive. Becky had to end things with her current boyfriend—but was Matthew willing to take his place?

WINGS OF CARE by Meredith Webber

Flying Doctors

Radio operator, Katy Woods, was secretly in love with Dr Peter Flint. So when he was trapped during a cyclone she willingly offered words of comfort. And on his return Peter made it clear that he wanted Katie! But did he want commitment?